Keep the Noise down, Kingsley

Also in the Totally Tom series:

Keep the Noise down, Kingsley

Jenny Oldfield

Illustrated by

Neal Layton

Hodder
Children's
Books

a division of Hodder Headline Limited

A Catalogue record for this book is available
from the British Library

ISBN 0 340 85105 8

Printed and bound in Great Britain

Hodder Children's Books
A Division of Hodder Headline Ltd
338 Euston Road
London NW1 3BH

One

Boom! Boom! Boom! Kingsley bashed the
big drum.

'Who let 'im loose?' Tom Bean clapped
his hands over his ears, waiting for his
friend to stop.

Boom-boom! Boom-boom! Boom-di-di-
boom!

'Ouch!' Wayne Penny cringed and
ran to the far side of the playground.

'My head hurts!'

'Very good, Kingsley!' Miss Ambler roared above the racket. 'Now, if we could just keep the noise level down a teenie-weenie bit...'

Boom-di-di-boom-boom! Kingsley marched up and down, left-right, left-right. He whacked the giant drum and strode along. At this rate, he would be mega well rehearsed for Saturday's procession. With Ryan beside him on cymbals and Kalid and Tom behind on trumpets, they would raise the roof on the town's new bandstand.

'Lovely, Kingsley!' Rambler Ambler trilled in her high, sing-song voice. 'Only, we must let the rest of the band get a look in every now and then.'

Kingsley reached the school gates and stopped. He turned like a soldier, head up, shoulders back, ready to begin again.

'STOP!' Tom darted forward to grab a drumstick. 'We can't hear ourselves think!'

In the background, the trombonists and

trumpeters stood with their fingers in their ears.

'Hey, give us that!' As Kingsley fought Tom for the drumstick he buffeted him with the drum and sent Tom crashing to the ground.

'Miss, he scratched my trumpet!' Tom claimed as he scrambled to his feet.

'Miss, he's deafening me!' Danielle Hazelwood cried. She, Bex Stevens, Sasha Jones and some other girls were rehearsing to be drum majorettes in the big procession.

'He's not even playing the right rhythm!' Bex complained. 'He's just banging it any old how!'

Tom sighed and shook his head. The trouble with Kingsley was that he never cared what anyone else thought. He did his own thing, full stop.

Boom-boom. Crash-bang. Left-right-left. The boy wonder was off again.

'Wait until I give you the signal!' Rambler called feebly. 'Kingsley, please try to remember that you're part of a team!'

'T-E-A-M!' Danielle spelled it out
scornfully. 'He doesn't understand the
meaning of the word. Gang leader; yes.
Front runner, captain, head of the crew,
top dude; definitely!'

'Leave him alone, he's having a good
time!' Lola Kidman grinned. Kingsley's
antics gave her time to practise a few
secret footie moves in the corner.

'Right, that's it!' Miss Ambler screeched.
She stormed across the playground after
Kingsley, who was still boom-booming like
mad. 'I forbid you to make another sound.
Stop it this instant!'

'Uh-oh, Rambler's lost it!' Kalid warned.
'This could be messy!'

But just then Mr Wright stepped in. 'It's
OK, leave this to me,' he told the young
teacher, having watched Kingsley ignore all
orders. In his tracksuit and trainers, fresh
from the soccer pitch, he stood across
drummer-boy's path and held his arms up

like a traffic cop. 'Hold it!' he ordered.

Boom-di-di...Kingsley stopped in mid-whack. 'What?'

'I said, hold it!' Leftie stood firm, deftly seizing both drumsticks from Kingsley. 'I can't think who let you loose with these!'

'Miss did,' Kingsley protested. 'She said I could play the drum in the street procession!'

'But that was before she realised that you and a giant drum could constitute a serious threat to public health,' Leftie pointed out. 'We'd have to issue everyone with a set of ear-muffs before we released you on to the streets of Woodbridge!'

'But sir!' Kingsley's broad smile was vanishing. 'Miss said I could!'

'Listen. Watch my lips. You, Kingsley Harris, will not be playing the drum on Saturday. As your form teacher, I know full well that you are the rowdiest kid in the school by a mile, and what's more that you've even been known to show off once in a while...'

'You're not kidding!' Bex, Sasha and Danielle muttered.

'For this reason, I have decided to shift you from the musical section of Saturday's event to a role more suited to your gifts and capabilities...'

'You're sacking me?' Kingsley's jaw dropped in disbelief.

'Too right!' Danielle agreed.

'No, Kingsley.' Firmly and calmly Leftie unstrapped the drum and let it rest on the tarmac. 'I want you to step sideways and take on the job of being in charge of the charity boxes.'

'Huh?'

'The tins we use to collect loose change from people in the crowd,' Leftie explained. 'The money goes to good causes, so you can see that it's very important for us to fill the tins as full as we can on the day. And I want you to head up that team!'

'Hmm.' Kingsley wasn't convinced. 'So

who gets to play the drum?'

Mr Wright turned to Miss Ambler, who cast a glance at the other gawping band members.

Eager hands shot up. 'Miss, me Miss! Miss, Miss!'

'Rebecca, you're a nice, sensible sort of person,' Rambler decided. 'Do you think you could learn to play the drum before the weekend?'

Bex flicked her light brown hair behind her shoulders then stepped forward. 'I think so, Miss Ambler!' she answered primly.

'Aw, Miss!' came the chorus from behind.

Ignoring the catcalls, the new drummer picked up her instrument, took the sticks from Leftie and stood ready.

Meanwhile, Tom sidled up to Kingsley. 'Bummer!' he whispered. Kingsley shrugged. 'No big deal.'

Boom-boom! Becky struck out at the front of the band.

'Tom Bean, pick up your trumpet and get

in line!' Rambler Ambler shrieked. 'To a
count of three!' the Music teacher told
them. 'One-two-three!'

Eeeek-boom-blare-wait-screech! The
band began to play a Viennese waltz.
Eek-boom-boom, squeak-boom-boom,
groan-boom-boom...

Bex marched ahead wielding her
drumsticks and drumming like a

demon, while Tom spat into his trumpet and Kingsley stood by, hands in pockets, quietly working out how he could still steal the show.

'OK, I'm gonna bust out the hardest trick I know!' Kingsley promised that night in the park. He threw his skateboard to the ground then scooted towards the vert.

'What's he gonna do?' Ryan whispered.

He, Tom, Wayne and Kalid had gathered to watch the crusha pull the rad move.

'Most likely his handplant,' Tom guessed. He knew that if Kingsley pulled this one without bailing...well, the dude was so sick he deserved to be in hospital!!

'Yo dude!' they cried. 'That's 100 per cent pure skateboarding!'

'Wow!' Kalid breathed.

'What's a handplant?' newcomer Wayne wanted to know.

'Hold your breath and watch,' Tom advised. He narrowed his eyes as Kingsley

began to pump up and down the ramp to
build up speed. As the skater neared the lip
at an angle, he stooped to grab the side of
his deck with his leading hand. Then, with
his trailing hand, he grabbed the top rim
of the ramp and flipped over into a one-
armed handstand.

'Shuuh!' Ryan gasped. Kingsley was
upside and turning his deck with his free
hand, keeping the turn going as he swung
back down on to the ramp, where he let go
of the grab and landed smoothly on all
four wheels.

'Sheez!' Wayne sighed.

'Yo dude!' Kalid and Tom cried. Only
Kingsley could've tried this and come out
in one piece.

The four watchers slammed their
decks on the hard ground to show their
admiration.

'Oi, keep the noise down!' someone
yelled from the garden of one of the
houses that overlooked the park. 'We're

trying to get a baby to sleep up here!'

'Top dude!' the crew yelled. 'K-I-N-G-S-L-E-Y, Kingsley!'

'Waaaagh!' the sleepless baby bawled.

'You kids, I'm warning you!' A fat, bald man in a bright yellow T-shirt and too-tight jeans appeared at the park gates. It was Angry Dad.

As Kingsley cruised past Tom and the

rest, he flashed them a grin. 'Again?' he boomed.

So the King of Hammett Street Park pulled the same sick trick to more hyped applause.

'Waaaaa-aaagh!' the babe with the leather lungs howled.

'K-I-N-G-S-L-E-Y!' The question had been answered. 'You are the King!'

By this time, Angry Dad had steam coming out of his ears. He was trucking down the grassy hill, saying he would strangle the skateboarders with his bare hands.

Tom rolled his eyes. 'What's he having a breakdown about?' he muttered.

'Dunno, but I'm not sticking around to find out,' Ryan decided, taking his deck and himself off towards the setting sun.

'Me neither,' Wayne agreed, scooting smoothly through the swing park towards the stone footbridge over the river.

'Keep your hair on!' Kingsley bellowed at Baldy-head, which set Tom and Kalid off like a couple of hyenas.

'Hey Kingsley!' a voice as loud as a foghorn blasted through the park.

'Waaa-aaagh!' Baldy's baby screamed blue murder.

'Uh-oh, that's my dad!' Kingsley grabbed his board. 'I was meant to be home for half-six to go see my gran. What time is it?'

'Ten past seven,' Kalid told him.

'My mum's gonna freak out big style.' The
usual grin was gone from Kingsley's face.

'What about your dad?' Tom saw that
Wesley Harris had appeared on the bridge.
The original foghorn voice was louder
than ever.

'No, Dad's cool. It's Mum who has the
nervous breakdowns.' Kingsley pulled a few
flashy 180 frontside slides then trucked on.
'I'm on my way!' he bellowed at Wesley.

'About beeping time!' Angry Dad arrived
puffing and panting. 'Don't you lot realise
that you're keeping half the kids in the
street awake?'

'It wasn't us!' Tom argued. His lightning
brain went into action and he pointed at
the disappearing Wayne and Ryan. 'It was
that kid with the fair hair, and the one
who copies dive-bombers, they made all
the noise!'

RULE NUMBER ONE: Always blame
somebody else.

'Was it heck as like!' Yellow T-shirt panted. 'I saw you all slamming those boards on the ground.'

Tom looked shiftily at the ground. 'Let's go!' he grunted at Kalid. There was obviously no point arguing.

'I'm out of here!' Kalid agreed.

With a rattle of trucks, the two set off for home.

'It makes no difference; I know who you are!' Angry Dad called after Tom. 'You're the postman's son. You live at Number 14!'

'Bummer!' Tom muttered as he skated rapidly away. That was information he'd rather have kept to himself. After all, there was a fair chance that Angry Dad was so wound up that he'd soon come knocking on the Beans' door.

'What's up with you?' his dad asked five minutes later, when Tom flopped down in front of *Corrie*.

'Nothin'!' Tom shot back.

'C'mon, what is it?' Harry turned down the volume and gave Tom a stare.

'Nothin'!' Rule Number One still lingered in Tom's head. 'It's just that Kingsley and his big mouth are gonna land us in trouble one of these days. I mean, like DEEP trouble!'

'Why, what's Kingsley done this time?' Trouble-alert sirens sounded for Harry Bean.

'Forget it,' Tom said, with an anxious glance out of the front-room window. No Angry Dad in sight; so far, so good. Maybe he was in the clear after all. Relax, chill out, enjoy, live to skate another day...'He's driving me nuts, that's all!'

Two

'Tom Bean, I hope you're not going to turn up tomorrow dressed like that!' Miss Ambler looked him up and down at the band's final, Friday night rehearsal.

Tom glanced down at his grey hoodie and baggy trousers. He wore his cap backwards, as always, plus shades and a chain looped from his side pocket.

'That's his cool skateboarding gear,'

Ryan pointed out.

'Precisely!' Ambler sniffed. 'But tomorrow, for the procession, I want everyone in strict school uniform!'

'Except us, Miss!' Danielle piped up.

The girls in the drum majorette section were prancing about in shiny, frilly skirts and white trainers. They carried giant pom-poms and yelled 'Ra-Ra-Ra!'

Behind Danielle's back, Lola stuck her fingers down her throat and mimed being sick.

'Lola!' Mr Wright warned. 'I saw that!'

'I wanna play the drum like Bex,' Lola complained. 'It's bad enough having to miss the match tomorrow, without having to dress up like Barbie!'

'Ah, but it's for a good cause!' Leftie reminded her.

'Ardilo's back in the team after his hamstring injury,' she muttered. To Lola, the Steelers' new signing was God.

'Watch it on Sky. Now go and strut your

stuff for Miss Ambler!' Leftie ordered.

'One more time!' Miss Boring Snoring cried. 'After three: one-two-three!'

Oom-pa-pa, oom-pa-pa! Woodbridge Junior School Band marched through the centre of town. Bex whacked the drum, Ryan clashed the cymbals and the rest trumpeted along. Ahead of the band, the girls tossed their pom-poms high in the air. Shoppers lined the pavements to watch the procession make its way through Fountain Square, past the Central Library and out towards Jubilee Park with its brand new bandstand.

'Wicked place to skateboard!' Ryan whispered to Tom, who had stopped playing to shake the spit out of the end of his trumpet.

'You wish!' Tom muttered back, eyeing the stone ramp leading up to the library. Hammett Street Park was the limit set by Beth and Harry Bean on Tom's skateboarding territory.

Boom-oom-pa, boom-oom-pa! Miss Ambler drove the troops on through the interested crowd.

'What's it all about?' one onlooker asked.

'They're opening the new bandstand,' someone replied.

'Nice day for it.'

'Woah, I can't hear myself think!'

Suddenly, Kingsley and his crew had burst into the square wearing highwayman masks. They rattled their collecting boxes in the faces of stunned shoppers.

'C'mon, give us yer money!' Kingsley roared. Chink-chink-chink! 'Dig in yer pockets, chuck your change in the box!'

'Anything to shut you up!' A man with a dog quickly coughed up his coins.

'Yeah, how many decibels is that?' A woman covered her toddler's ears to protect him.

'Yer money or yer life!' Kingsley swashbuckled his way through the crowd, out-roaring the drum and the trumpets.

Clunk-clunk! People slid coins through the slot just to give their ears a rest.

'Not a kid you could easily ignore,' a traffic warden commented, dropping his coins in the nearest box.

'C'mon, empty yer pockets! Hand over everything you've got, or you're dead men!' Kingsley insisted at the top of his foghorn voice.

'I'm not sure about his methods,' the traffic warden grumbled as he dug deeper.

'Good luck to him,' a white-haired lady smiled. 'He's doing a grand job, bless him!'

Kingsley and his masked men rampaged on through the square, their tins weighed down with plunder. 'Yer money or yer life!' they bellowed. 'Don't be tight, give us all you've got!'

'Erm, Kingsley, whose idea were the masks?' Mr Wright asked quietly, once the bandstand had been opened by the Lord Mayor and everyone was drinking cups of tea in the big marquee.

Tom stood nearby to hear Kingsley wriggle out of this one.

'Mine, sir!'

Leftie nodded thoughtfully. 'It was your idea to employ the strong-arm tactics as well, I suppose?'

'Yes, sir!' Kingsley beamed proudly. He twirled his highwayman mask between his thumb and forefinger.

'And don't you think that it was perhaps a bit OTT?'

'No, sir. It worked, didn't it?' He chinked his full tin under Leftie's nose. 'We collected loads of dosh!'

'Yes, and you managed to drown out the band and steal the limelight from the majorettes in the process!'

Kingsley didn't reply, but he raised his eyebrows and stared, as if to say, 'Who, me?'

Kingsley United one, Rambler Ambler nil, Tom decided. Serves her right for

'But the main point is, you didn't ask Miss Ambler for permission,' Leftie pointed out. 'It took her completely by surprise because of course she was much too busy conducting the band to notice what you were up to.'

'Yes sir, sorry sir.' Kingsley didn't meet Leftie's gaze.

'You don't look it.'

'I am, sir; honest, sir!'

'Miss Ambler's very upset. She thinks the masks are out of keeping with the image the school wants to convey. She's nervous about people's reactions.'

Yeah, she's scared it'll get back to Waymann and she'll get the blame! Tom thought.

'Does she want us to give the money back?' Kingsley asked, dead innocent, and seemingly willing to help.

Like how? Tom wondered. Then he realised Kingsley was having the last

Leftie narrowed his eyes. 'Don't push your luck,' he warned. 'Listen, Kingsley, take some advice. If I were you, I'd keep a low profile on Monday, until people in school have forgotten about the Dick Turpin act. Y'know the sort of thing–show up on time, hand your homework in, stand in line, don't run in the corridors...'

Kingsley nodded, put his hand up to cough and gave Tom a secret grin. *I got away with it. Yo dude!*

'Oh, and Kingsley...' Leftie had turned away but came back with a final word of warning. 'Keep the noise down in future, huh?'

Monday came, and Tom's class had a lesson on Exploring the Environment.

'The environment is whatever we can see around us,' Leftie explained. 'Trees, the river, the old stone footbridge...'

'Skateboard park!' Tom snuck in.

Thirty kids and one teacher stood in Hammett Street Park exploring the environment. It was cold, windy and wet. Everyone was miserable.

Leftie ignored Tom. 'The footbridge across the river was actually built as a crossing for packhorses in the sixteenth century, long before the town had the modern road bridge. I want you to come and see how the stone has been worn away by the weather and by the horses' hooves.'

'Clip-clop, clip-clop!' Kingsley ran ahead over the bridge, slapping his thigh and neighing. The wind caught his tie and flapped it in his face, so he reared up and whinnied.

'Yes, thank you, Kingsley!' Leftie called, but not before a stampede of wild horses had followed the leader over the bridge.

'Yee-hah!' Tom gave a cowboy yell, followed by a Native American war cry. 'Kerpow!' he drew his six-shooter from its holster, aimed and fired.

Leftie pressed on. 'To the right of the bridge are the remains of stepping stones used by monks on their way to Farfield Abbey.'

In a flash, Kingsley had charged unseen down to the river bank and jumped on to the first flat stepping stone.

'Come back, it's dangerous!' Danielle called.

'A load of old monks could do it, couldn't they?' Kingsley retorted.

'Yeah!' Tom agreed, landing nimbly beside him. The river rushed to either side of the mossy stone, lapping at his trainers. He didn't notice Kingsley beat a hasty retreat to the bank before Danielle grabbed Leftie's attention and pointed an accusing finger towards Tom.

'Tom Bean, get off that stone!' the panicky teacher yelled.

Tom looked round to find himself all alone.

'That's just the sort of lunatic trick I'd

expect from you, Tom! Jump back on to the bank right now!'

Tom jumped. 'Thanks a lot!' he hissed at Kingsley, cleverly hidden behind a tree.

'Don't blame me, it was Danielle who dobbed you in,' Kingsley told him, cheerfully galloping on.

'Sir, Kingsley jumped in a puddle and splashed me!' Sasha cried.

Bex had joined in the complaints. 'Sir, he's made me soaking wet!'

'Kingsley, you're driving everyone crazy,' Leftie told him before the rain-soaked group returned to school. 'Didn't you listen to a word I said on Saturday?'

Kingsley put on his why-what-did-I-do? expression—big eyes, open mouth, high shoulders. He'd been plugged into his Walkman, grooving to a rhythm.

Now it was Tuesday; a new day but the same old Kingsley.

'Owzat!' he cried, diving full length to

take a catch on the cricket pitch. Then he jumped up, throwing the ball sky high.

'Not out!' Lola protested by digging her bat firmly into the crease. 'The ball bounced before he caught it.'

Kingsley charged the umpire. 'Out!' he bellowed. 'The ball never bounced. I caught her, she's O-U-T, out!'

'God, Kingsley, you so get on my nerves!' Bex sighed. 'It's only a stupid cricket match, not World War Three!'

'Calm down,' Leftie told them. 'Lola's not out, Kingsley. I'm the umpire, so my decision is final.'

'Nah-nah!' Sasha chipped in. She was batting at the other end of the pitch to Lola. 'We're thirty-three for four. We're gonna beat you, Kingsley!'

Sulking, Kingsley took up position in between Ryan and Wayne. Tom took his run-up then bowled. Lola stabbed at the ball with her bat, missed and heard the wickets tumble.

'OWZZZAAAT!' Kingsley roared. He lunged at Ryan and flung his arms around him, then danced towards the wicket. 'CLEAN BOWLED. THIRTY-THREE FOR FIVE!'

'Yeah, yeah, they can hear you in Australia!' Lola muttered, stomping past on her way to the edge of the pitch. 'Anyway, you're for it now, Kingsley,' she added, jabbing her bat towards Bernie King and Fat Lennox.

The caretaker and his dog came waddling across the playing field with a message from Mrs Waymann. 'The Head says to keep the noise down out here,' Bernie wheezed. 'She's showing some important visitors around the school. You all have to be on your best behaviour!'

As he talked, Lennox went sniffing up to Tom.

'Get down!' Tom didn't want the bulldog's slobbery chops near him, so he hid the cricket ball in his tracksuit pocket and backed away.

'OK.' Leftie received Bernie's message loud and clear. 'We'll make sure we play more quietly.'

'I'd like to know who was making all that noise,' the caretaker growled, casting his beady eye around the pitch and letting it rest on Tom. Kingsley meanwhile had faded quietly into the background.

'Naff off!' Tom hissed at Slobber Chops, who had just poked his blunt nose into Tom's pocket. He shoved him away with his hand.

Sniff-sniff, slobber-slobber. The dog wanted that cricket ball.

Tom saw Lennox open his jaws. His teeth were sharp as a shark's, his tongue pink and slavery.

Wumph! The jaws snapped shut and Lennox had a mouthful of Tom's tracksuit.

'GER'IM OFF ME!' Tom screamed.

All eyes swivelled towards him, but not fast enough to see Lennox let go and slink away.

'Huh, I might've known!' Bernie grunted, overlooking Lennox's part in the action. 'Tom Bean's been opening his big mouth as usual.'

'B-b-but!' Tom protested, before a glance from Fat Lennox silenced him.

Tom turned to Kingsley, waiting for him to own up, but Kingsley stuck his head in the air and gazed up at the clouds.

'Don't worry, now that I know who the culprit is I'll pass the name on to Mrs Waymann,' Bernie announced. 'I'll tell her it's Tom Bean up to his tricks, causing a riot out here. I'm sure she'll be wanting a little word with him after her visitors have gone.'

Thanks a million, Kingsley! Tom ground his teeth and kept quiet. Until the dog had sunk its teeth into his tracksuit, Tom hadn't made a peep! But then, you couldn't dob in a mate. So silently he watched Fat Lennox trundle off after Bernie King.

Yeah, he thought. *Three times in three days Kingsley has dropped me in it. First* with Angry Dad, second down on the stepping stones with Leftie, and now with Bernie and the Head. This isn't funny. In fact, it's definitely freaking me out. I gotta do something about it—and fast!

Three

It was time for a heart-to-heart with Chippie.

'It's not like I hate Kingsley or anything,' Tom confided in the bird. 'It's just that he's mega annoying.'

'Chip-chippety-chip!' *How come?* The blue budgie cosied up against Tom's cheek. All around, yellow, green and blue birds preened and fluttered.

'Well, for a start, he's a big show-off.'

'Chippety-chip.' *In what way?* The budgie ducked his head and blinked his beady eyes.

'He always has to be the main man,' Tom sighed, looking absently around his dad's shed. He liked it here, talking to his favourite bird. It was warm and cosy, full of chattering, living things. 'Like, for instance, Miss Ambler takes him off the drum because he's drowning out the rest of the band, but he still manages to be the kid everyone looks at.'

So what? Get over it, was Chippie's advice.

'Plus he keeps on dropping me in it.' Tom had been hauled in front of Waymann after school.

'Mr King tells me that you were the rowdy one out on the cricket pitch this afternoon.' The Head had obviously had a bad day with her special visitors. Her forehead was criss-crossed with wrinkles and she looked

like she'd been sucking lemons.

Tom had frowned back. 'Lennox ripped my pocket.'

Waymann gave him a long, hard stare. 'Which pocket? Show me.'

'My tracksuit pocket, Miss.' OK so the pocket wasn't actually ripped...Tom shifted uneasily from foot to foot.

'Typical!' Mrs Waymann shook her head. 'When you're in trouble, Tom, you always try to lay the blame at someone else's door!'

'It's true, Miss. I had to yell; Lennox was sinking his teeth into my leg!'

'So you're admitting you were the culprit.' Witchy Waymann revved herself up to give Tom a lecture. 'Cricket is only a game...don't get carried away...self-control...manners...

image of the school is damaged...
blah-di-blah.'

In the end, she'd let Tom off with a
warning. 'Any more of this rowdy behaviour
and I'll have to think very seriously about
banning you from our school sports teams!'

No, not that! Tom lived for footie (and
skateboarding). The threat had struck him
dumb for once.

Waymann had skewered him with
her mean stare one last time, then sent
him home.

'Kebabbed!' Tom groaned at Chippie.
'Left wriggling on a spike. And all down
to Kingsley.'

That's life. 'Who's a cheeky boy? Chip-
chip-chippety-chip!'

The budgie did a little dance on Tom's
shoulder. *Get out there, dude, and do
your thing!*

'Thomas!' Beth Bean called from the
kitchen door. 'I want you to run down to
the shop and fetch some milk!'

'I'm outta here!' Tom told Chippie, sneaking out of the back gate before his mum could collar him.

'Tom–milk!' Beth yelled.

But he was gone, with his skateboard under his arm. Like Chippie said, get out there and do your thing.

'I'm gonna nail this trick if it kills me!' Tom concentrated one hundred per cent on pulling off a heelflip followed by a boardslide along the park railing. He bit his bottom lip, crouched forward and used his arms to balance.

Slam! He toppled from the rail and hit the ground. His pro-board was starting to split nicely, but it would still take a good few bails to make it look really sick.

'Stand back!' Kingsley tried the same move and pulled it with ease.

'Gnarly!' Ryan yelled, as Kingsley's deck slid down the rail with the trucks hanging either side. The crew of Ryan, Kalid, Lola

and Wayne skated down the hill beside their main man.

'Huh!' Tom tried again. This time, the move worked perfectly, but there was no one around to see.

'Hey, Kingsley, how fast can you go up the ramp?' Lola challenged.

'Thirty miles an hour; watch!' The speed king zoomed along, left foot forward. When he reached the rim of the ramp, he ollied over the far side.

'Vroom!' Kalid was impressed.

'Take a look at this!' Tom decided to follow on with a radical, speed demon trick where he flung himself flat on his belly and clocked up probably 40mph. OK, so he winded himself when he landed, but it was a sick move.

'Splat!' Kingsley crowed over Tom's spreadeagled body. 'Watch you don't bust something pulling tricks like that!'

'Hmm.' As soon as he could breathe again, Tom took his board off to a quiet part of the park where he could practise in peace. Let Kingsley have all the glory; see if he cared. According to the pro-skateboarder, Justin Valentine, from a quote in Tom's latest *Crusha* magazine, 'Skateboarding's not about who's number one. It's about having fun.' Tom chanted this to himself now.

'We are the champions!' The Hammett Park loudmouth let off steam with a football chant. 'We shall not, we shall not be moved!'

The crew joined in, 'We will win the FA Cup, we shall not be moved.'

'Waaa-aagh!' Their noise had woken the baby.

'Not again!' Tom tutted, still managing to perfect a high kickflip. Then he watched the usual routine from a distance; the appearance of Angry Dad, the shouting and yelling, the wailing baby.

'We are the champions of the world!' Kingsley bellowed.

'I'll give you champions!' Baldy retorted, then disappeared back into his house.

Tom chose a kerb along the edge of the riverside path. He planned to grind as far along it as he could. But before he could ollie on to it, a car came speeding down Hammett Street and stopped at the park gates.

Suddenly, everything went quiet. The silence made Tom glance up–just in time to see Kalid, Ryan, Lola, Wayne and Kingsley scatter and sprint away.

Slowly the white car turned in through the wide gates, and now Tom could make out the neon-bright orange stripe and the blue light on top.

Cops! Angry Dad must've called them. Two uniforms were getting out of the car, right now, and heading Tom's way...

...Which was how come Tom landed up back at his house with a police escort.

'He was definitely one of them!' Angry

Dad claimed at the park, totally mad at
the police for letting the others scarper.
'Every single night he's here with his
skateboarding mates, kicking up a racket.
Me and the wife, we're sick to death of it!'
   And the woman officer told Tom
that there were other complaints. 'You
lot need to keep a lid on things. Haven't
you heard of noise pollution? There's a

law against it, y'know!'

'You mean, we can get arrested for shouting and stuff? Tom had been shaking in his trainers.

'If it annoys the neighbours, and you do it often enough...' The second police officer glanced after the vanishing figures of Kingsley and the rest. 'Looks like they left you to carry the can.'

So what's new? Tom had shrugged. And the shrug had annoyed Angry Dad, who then told the cops where Tom lived. 'Take him home and tell his parents what he gets up to when they let him out at night. These kids will be running wild in a year or two unless the family steps in and nips it in the bud!'

'Keep an eye on him,' the woman officer told Beth and Harry, back at Tom's house. Beth nodded and thanked the officer, while Tom squirmed and hung his head.

'He wasn't the only one, but the others scarpered as soon as they saw our car. Your boy was unlucky in that he didn't spot us in time,' the officer went on.

Harry thanked her and said they were very sorry that Tom had caused trouble with the neighbours. 'It won't happen again,' he promised...

...Which meant no more skateboarding in the park after five o'clock.

'You can't be serious!' Tom whinged.

'Dead serious,' Harry insisted.

'Why?'

'Because!' Tom's dad wouldn't take any more arguments.

'Kingsley will still be there until half-seven!' Tom's attempt to point out the flaw in the new ruling went unheeded. 'Mum, Dad, listen! Kingsley makes more noise than me. He can't help it, it's the way he is!'

'We're not interested in what Kingsley gets up to,' Beth told him.

Tom grew desperate. 'A jumbo jet makes

more noise than me, and they don't ban them! Or somebody mowing the lawn, or a car radio blasting out–everything!'

But his mum and dad weren't listening. Tom had a 5pm curfew, and that was that.

'Never mind.' After three miserable days of Tom having to stay in and watch *Neighbours*, Wayne tried to cheer him up. 'I've asked my mum if I can go skateboarding in Jubilee Park tomorrow and she said yes!'

'So?' Tom jinxed Kingsley as he skated by after the end of Friday school. *Fall off and twist your ankle!* he willed. But the Main Man wove effortlessly across the playground.

'Cheer up, Tom; it's the weekend,' Mr Wright called as he got ready to set off home on his motorbike.

'So, d'you wanna come?' Wayne asked.

'Not allowed,' Tom answered bluntly. The mood his mum and dad were in, there was no chance.

'What if my mum asks your mum for you?'

Tom sniffed.

'Come on, Tom. I owe you!'

True; when shy Wayne had first come to the school, Tom had done loads of stuff to help him settle in, including rescuing him from a cubicle in the boys' toilets.

'I mean, we can skate around the lake and up into the new bandstand. It'll be cool!'

'Yeah, rad,' Tom agreed. He glimpsed himself pulling sick moves in front of a gawping crowd of picnickers and passers-by. Big temptation! Like, mega!

'Shall I get her to ask?' Wayne was fixing the peak of his cap and putting on his shades.

Tom gave in to the vision of himself slipping, sliding, jumping and grinding in the centre of town. After all, Wayne Penny was one of the quietest kids around, and

Wayne's mum, Jo, was Beth's keep-fit friend. Surely his own mum would have to agree.

'Yeah!' he grinned, giving Wayne a high five salute. 'Tomorrow, Jubilee Park. You and me, dude!'

Four

The double decker bus rattled and
swayed along City Road past the Steelers'
ground. Tom and Wayne sat on top at the
very front, taking in every detail of the
new stand.

'Rows of blue and white seats!' Wayne
pointed out.

'They're for the season ticket holders.
Hey, look at that statue of Billy Jennings!'

Tom jumped up and pointed at the life-size bronze figure of one of the all-time footballing greats from the 1960s. Billy stood by the entrance to the new stand, his empty metal gaze surveying the gravel car park beyond the turnstiles.

'Yeah, I read about it on the club website. Billy's widow unveiled it at the end of last season.' Wayne's attention was on the traffic jam ahead. 'At this rate we're never gonna get there!'

Tom knew he was jammy to have made it this far. Flashback to yesterday tea time:

Harry (munching crispy fried bread): Who was that on the phone?

Beth (coming back to her place at the table): Jo Penny.

(Tom suddenly sits up straight and earwigs hard.)

Harry: About your aerobics class?

Beth (thoughtfully): No, actually. It was about Wayne going skateboarding in Jubilee Park tomorrow morning.

Jo wondered if Tom could go with him.

(Tom holds his breath and secretly crosses his fingers underneath the table.)

Harry: Did you tell her Tom was semi-grounded?

Beth (nodding): But Jo seemed pretty keen. Reading between the lines, I'm guessing that she's nervous about Wayne going by himself. You know what he's like; dead shy and quiet. She probably thinks he could get picked on in the city centre. Plus, he's still fairly new to the area.

Harry: Huh, and she thinks Tom is sensible enough to look out for Wayne?

(Tom winces. It hurts when his mild-mannered dad has a go at him.)

Beth: Apparently. I did try to explain why Tom was living under a dark cloud of suspicion at the moment...

Tom (under his breath): Mmmrgh-grr-sss-s'not fair!

Harry: So what did you decide?

Beth: Said I'd ring her back when I'd

talked to you about it.

(All this while, Tom's head turns to and fro, like a spectator at a tennis match.)

Nick (Tom's older brother, who has been chomping his burger and slurping a can of Coke meanwhile): You realise Big Lugs can hear every word you're saying?

Beth: Yeah, Tom, go and see to the birds while we finish discussing this.

Tom (scraping his chair back noisily and scowling at Nick): Remind me to put rat poison in your Coke next time!

Tom had stomped out to the shed and grumbled to the budgies. 'Mmm-grr-beeping Nick!'

Chill out, Chippie had said. 'Where's Thomas? Who's a cheeky boy?'

After a quarter of an hour of scratching and scraping at the tiny piles of grey bird muck on the shed floor, Tom had ventured back inside the house.

His mum and dad had been washing up

in the kitchen, and Nick had been the first one Tom met up with.

'Tough, kiddo!' Nick had flicked out at Tom with the end of a soggy tea-towel. 'No parkies for Tommy tomorrow, diddums!'

Tom head-butted his brother in the stomach for this.

'Stop fighting, you two.' Beth broke it up. 'Nick, do you have to wind Tom up all the time?'

'Can I go?' Tom emerged from the scrap with messy hair and a red face.

'On one condition,' his mum had insisted. 'No; two. First, that you're back for lunch, and second that you absolutely, cross-your-heart-and-hope-to-die promise not to lead poor Wayne astray!'

Jammy, or what? Tom grinned to himself at the sob-story Wayne must have told Jo Penny. 'Don't wanna go by myself–Tom Bean's the best skater in the school (well, maybe not this bit)–he's my mate.' Worry-guts Jo would've bought it big time. 'Well, Wayne, I'm really not happy about you going alone anyway. Let me give Beth a call and see what we can arrange...'

Now Wayne fretted about the traffic and the bus inched forward.

'C'mon, let's go!' Tom leaped up and scrambled for the stairs. Down two at a time, buzzing for the next stop, tumbling out on to the pavement in full skateboarding gear.

'We can skate to Fountain Square faster than the bus can drop us there,' he explained.

'Hey, Mosha!' a kid across the street yelled.

Tom was glad he'd worn his Slipknot hoodie and baggiest trousers. With his board under his arm and a heavy chain dangling from his pocket, he held his head up high.

Soon he and Wayne had coasted smoothly along the pavement into the town centre. Jubilee Park lay across town, beyond Fountain Square which was busy with Saturday morning shoppers. Tom glanced longingly at the long ramp with low railings leading up to the Central Library and the Marshway Shopping Centre beyond.

He stopped by the tall sparkling fountain. 'We could pull a wicked grind down there!' he pointed out to Wayne.

Wayne shook his head. 'No way!'

'Why not?'

'I promised Mum we'd only skate in the park.'

Tom tutted. 'How come?' That ramp was mega tempting.

'Mum says you get moved on by the police if you skate round here.' Wayne's wide blue eyes took on a worried look.

'Yeah, that's only if you get caught.' Trucking through a crowd of fat pigeons squatting on the flags beyond the fountain, Tom gave way to temptation.

The pigeons squawked and fluttered. A dog ran across the square and chased them. An attendant inside the library spotted Tom's approach, came out through the sliding doors and collared him.

'Not here, you don't!' he growled. He made as if to grab Tom's board.

Tom wrestled it back. 'OK, OK!' he muttered. 'Keep your hair on.' He always said this to bald, middle-aged geezers because he knew it annoyed them big time.

The attendant glowered. 'Cheeky monkey!'

Tom grinned, slapped down his board and pulled a quick board slide down the railing. He joined Wayne at the bottom of the ramp. Together they scooted across the square.

'Told you!' Wayne gasped.

Tom grinned. He'd pulled his grind, and that was what mattered.

Now for the park.

In through the big iron gates, along footpaths towards the new bandstand. Weaving among parents pushing pushchairs, old men with walking sticks, other kids heading for the skate park section, Tom led Wayne. There were bright red and yellow tulips standing to attention in flowerbeds, trees overhanging a narrow stream, a boating pond and an ice-cream kiosk surrounded by tables and chairs.

'Cool!' Tom tic-tacked around a sign

pointing to Crazy Golf, shot off in that direction and skated over the tiny ramps and banks that made up the course. Then he was off again, with a breathless Wayne in tow, past some tennis courts until they reached the skate park.

'Wow!' Wayne bailed in astonishment. Ahead of him he saw ramps and obstacles he'd only ever dreamed about. There was a bright sign saying 'Skatetastic!' and a bunch of moshas standing in line to skate the course.

There was a quarter-pipe and a half-pipe, a roll-in bank and a fly-off ramp for big airs. A kerb block with metal coping ran the length of one side of the course.

Tom recognised them all from the videos he'd studied, but this was the first time he'd met up with them in real life.

'Look at that bowl!' he muttered, blowing out air like a boxer getting ready to punch. He saw a kid jump the queue and get pushed back to the end, then the next skater set off.

'What do we do now?' Wayne asked in a jittery voice.

'Stand in line and watch.' Tom knew it was important to pull the moves in your head before you tried them. Skateboarding was sixty per cent concentration, only forty per cent action.

'They're all bigger than us!' Wayne whispered.

'So?' Tom pressed his shades firmly on to

his nose and swaggered across. He was
ready to rock and roll and taste the air!

*It's not about winning, it's about
having fun!* he told himself as his turn
drew nearer.

*Yeah, but you fall flat on your face and it
doesn't look good, dude!* a voice inside his
head warned him. It sounded like the sort
of thing Chippie would say.

I can do this, easy!

*You know what they say about the
pride thing.*

I'm good!

How good?

*I've watched the pros pull the moves in
slow motion, frame by frame.*

*Yeah, but those guys on the video
probably slammed ten times before they
got it right.*

It was Tom's turn next and his inner voice
was really getting to him. But one glance at
Wayne told Tom that if he was nervous,
then Wayne was petrified. 'You'll be OK.

Just take it low and slow,' he muttered as they shuffled forward one last time.

Wayne took a deep breath. When he nodded, his teeth rattled big time.

This was it. Tom's turn. Everyone's eyes were glued on him. First, a noseslide along the kerb, them pumping up the ramp, making sure he hit the trannie exactly right. After that, he hit the coping at an angle, flipped his deck and introduced a dark side slide.

Bam! The onlookers slammed their boards on to the ground. Well cool!

So Tom relaxed and started to enjoy himself, pulling a rock fakie and remembering to lean back as he rolled. Flexing his knees, balancing with his arms, he went from good to excellent, ending with a fakie tail stall where he rode his stick backwards up the ramp at top speed then pushed down on the tail to stop the whole thing dead.

Wicked! The slammers thrashed their

boards on the tarmac.

'Who is that kid?'

'How old is he?'

'Where did he learn to skate?'

Tom beamed then stood back to watch his shy friend.

Wayne chose a slower, steadier course, concentrating hard. He crouched forward, his cap jammed down, fair hair flopping over his forehead.

Don't bail! Tom kept his fingers crossed. *Stick with it, you can do it!* This meant as much to Tom as it did to Wayne.

Wayne wobbled along the kerb but made it. He gathered speed up the first ramp and ollied clear.

Don't fall flat, don't lose it! Tom prayed.

And Wayne made it, turning his board beneath him, throwing in a 180 kickturn for good measure. The watching crew slammed their boards in encouragement.

'The kid's OK.'

'He's got guts!'

Tom grinned again, sprinting up to Wayne at the finish of the course. He raised his hand in a high-five.

'We're one pair of cool dudes!' he beamed. 'C'mon, let's do it one more time!'

Five

Tom and Wayne. Wayne and Tom. We're the main men!

Together they'd stood the test.

'Wicked!' Wayne whispered as they coasted through Fountain Square. His pale face glowed with happiness, his eyes were lit up with pride.

Tom said nothing. He was reliving the heart-stopping moment when he'd pulled his fakie tail stall; the split-second timing, the gasp from the crowd.

'Whassup!' a voice bellowed. A dark figure came hurtling down the library ramp. 'Beanie Babe, Henny Penny, whaaa-aassup!'

'Oh no, Kingsley!' Tom stopped by the fountain. 'What's he doing here?'

Wayne nipped out of the way as the Loud Mouth King sped towards them.

Kingsley scattered the fat pigeons and thin dogs. His trucks roared over the flagstones, his black hoodie billowed in the wind.

Kingsley in black baggies and Emerica trainers with the tongues spewing out. A gruesome, piratical sight with his death's head design across his chest and red bandanna around his head.

'Hey, watch it!'

'Flippin' 'eck!'

'Bloomin' kids!'

'Hey Kingsley,' Tom muttered as the big show-off screeched around the rim of the fountain. He still hadn't forgiven him for scarpering from Hammett Street Park.

'We just went to Skatetastic!' Wayne announced. 'You should've come!'

'Nah, it's loads better skating round here,' Kingsley declared, plugging himself into his Walkman, then casually grinding around the low concrete wall surrounding the fountain. He ollied back to ground level with casual ease.

No doubt about it; Kingsley was good. Tom scowled deeply.

'You know you're not allowed!' Wayne reminded him.

Kingsley laughed. 'Yeah, I ran into the gorilla from the library! Hey you two wanna pump up the ramp and grind down the rail with me?' he spoke extra loud because of the music blasting into his ears.

Timid Wayne shook his head.

'Cluck-cluck-cluck!' Kingsley flapped his arms like a chicken.

'Yeah!' Tom decided instantly. Nobody

flapped their wings at him!

'B-b-but!' Wayne began. He stopped, looked around wildly, then pointed to the clock tower on the Marshway Shopping Centre. 'It's twelve o'clock. I told Mum I'd be back.'

'Just one go,' Tom promised, scooting off alongside Kingsley.

'I don't think we should!' Wayne gasped, running hard to keep up.

'What's up, Wayne? Don't be a wimp!' As he flung this remark over his shoulder, Tom was struck by the memory of his mum laying down the law before he came to town.

Two conditions, she'd said. First, be back for lunch. Second, don't lead Wayne astray!

Tom felt a fleeting pang of conscience and almost stopped. But Kingsley was racing on, pumping up the ramp, right under the nose of the library door attendant. 'You wait here,' he hissed at Wayne. 'I won't be a sec!'

So Wayne waited, while Tom and Kingsley
broke every rule in the book.

Bold as brass they zigzagged up the wide
slope, Kingsley still plugged into his mosha
music, Tom darting in between people
laden with library books. At the top of the
ramp, the glass doors slid silently open and
Gorilla Man appeared.

'I've told you before!' he yelled, red

in the face with rage.

But the two skaters ignored him, swooping around 180 degrees and facing downhill. Tom was first to ollie up on to the rail and pull a neat k-grind which kept the weight on his front foot and the back truck in the air.

Wheeee! He slid like greased lightning, thirty miles per hour, easy.

Tom heard Kingsley follow. 'Yeah!' Kingsley yelled. 'Neee-yaaah, Geronimo!'

Quickly Tom bailed at the end of the rail and jumped to one side. Kingsley was speeding down with a straight 50-50, both trucks straddling the rail. He looked wicked, as good as a pro, leaving the mottled attendant opening and closing his mouth like a stranded trout.

But for once, Kingsley failed to pull the perfect move. He was so busy yelling out the lyrics of his song–'I wanna, wanna, wanna be there, baby!'–that he forgot to push down on the kicktail to come safely off the end of the rail.

'Sixty per cent concentration, forty per cent action,' Tom repeated grimly as he watched Kingsley make big air across Fountain Square.

'Oi, sonny, where's your brake?' an old man called.

Kingsley raised the pigeons and stormed on. Across the flagstones towards the covered entrance of the shopping centre, straight between the open doors.

'Uh-oh!' Tom glanced at Wayne, who watched open-mouthed.

'Kingsley Harris, aged nine-and-a-half, last seen vanishing into Marshway at 12.05, dressed in a black hoodie and a red bandanna. Woodbridge police have put out a call for his arrest. They wish to interview Harris for serious speeding offences!'

'Nee-yah!' Enjoying himself now, Kingsley shot ahead, across the main walkway, knocking shoppers aside like skittles.

'Oh no!' Wayne breathed.

'C'mon, we'd better go after him,' Tom decided. He expected that sooner or later, they would have to scrape the speed demon off the floor.

So he and Wayne tucked their boards under their arms and sprinted into the shopping centre, in time to see Kingsley grind down an escalator rail, into Marks and Spencer's food hall.

In amongst the lettuces and cucumbers, his Walkman blasting, Kingsley wore a big smile. Through the Cakes and Biscuits section, before Security could stop him, he made a beeline for the Delivery exit.

In their eagerness to keep up, Wayne and Tom got stuck in a queue for the till. They escaped in time to see the happy show-off sail out of the back entrance and disappear down a dark ramp.

'He's for it this time!' Wayne sighed, while Tom sprinted on.

The delivery door led on to a giant basement car park where M&S wagons shunted to and from half a dozen delivery bays. It just so happened that Kingsley's bay was empty, thank heavens.

Tom looked around the loading and unloading area, trying to make out where their so-called mate had got to now. Behind him, a kerfuffle beyond the double doors told him that they were being followed.

'Where is he?' Wayne peered into the

gloom of the concrete depot.

'Disappeared in a puff of smoke!' Tom grunted. Typical Kingsley, leaving them to take the rap! 'Yeah, we should've left him to it!'

While he grumbled and looked for cover, Wayne noticed an empty lorry in the bay next door draw up its metal ramp, ready to leave. As soon as the back had clunked shut, the driver eased his vehicle forward and trundled towards a square of daylight and the big wide world beyond.

'Tom-om!' Wayne's voice wavered.

'What?' At this rate, the two of them would get nicked and they'd be in deep trouble. Tom would've led Wayne astray. He'd be permanently grounded, like forever!!

Wayne drew a deep breath and pointed to the departing lorry. 'You don't think...?'

Tom frowned. One kid on a skateboard. One ramp. One open door into the back of a truck...

'Maybe there was a lorry here in this bay when Kingsley shot through the door!' Wayne gasped.

Oh no! Tom groaned silently. Kingsley shooting on to the metal ramp and landing inside the lorry. The back door being raised, the driver setting off...

'He could be on his way to the motorway, right now, this very minute!' Tom was the one who voiced their fears.

Kingsley pounding on the sides of the empty lorry, heading who knew where!

Six

'Hey, you two, what d'you think you're doing?' A woman in an M&S uniform appeared in the doorway behind Tom and Wayne. 'This area is private. You're not allowed out here.'

Tom backed up against a nearby concrete pillar. 'We were just...We've lost...I mean, we're...out of here!' he decided.

Grabbing Wayne, he jumped down into

the well of the loading area. 'Scarper!' he ordered, slamming down his board and skating towards the wide exit on to the street.

Their trucks trundled over the rough, oil-slicked concrete–slow going, but Tom knew that the nicely dressed member of staff wouldn't follow them. Instead, she would call for help, and by the time it arrived Tom and Wayne would be long gone.

So he wasn't expecting the yellow metal pole that descended across the exit, nor the tall security guard who stepped out in front of them.

'Hold it!' The man held up his hand like a traffic cop.

'Duck!' Tom yelled at Wayne.

They were safely under the barrier and swerving around the guard, taking the slope down the street that ran round the back of the store, with the angry guard shaking his fist after them.

'Take a left!' Tom ordered. He swung around the corner at top speed, glanced back to check that Wayne had made it, then coasted on.

'We made it!' Wayne caught him up and skated alongside. By now they were heading back towards the shopping centre, taking another left in through a side door where they could mingle with the crowds.

'Yeah, we made it.' Tom relaxed. He noted that Wayne's eyes were alive with the danger and excitement of what they'd just been through.

'But what about poor Kingsley?' Wayne added.

Poor Kingsley-nothing! The Walkman King had just pulled a crazy stunt and almost landed Wayne and Tom right in it-again! For a while, Tom felt like shrugging his shoulders and walking away.

'What are we gonna tell everyone?' Wayne groaned. He dodged a gang of girls parading towards them, then went on with his line of thought. 'I mean, Kingsley's stuck in a lorry and we have to let people know. Like, his mum and dad for instance!'

'I guess.' Tom didn't want to be the one who broke the bad news.

'Think about it,' Wayne insisted. 'What happens when Kingsley doesn't show up for his dinner? Mr and Mrs Harris will think he's been mugged, or had an accident!'

Tom stopped to stare in the sports shop window. There were some cool trainers and a new style of cap to drool over.

'Tom!' Wayne waved a hand in front of Tom's face. 'Hello, anybody home? I'm asking, what are we gonna do about Kingsley? He could be in Scotland by now, for all we know!'

'Yeah, or hey, he could be freezing to death inside a giant freezer, if the lorry he skated into was carrying frozen food!' As this thought took hold in Tom's head, he began to worry big style.

Clunk! The heavy door had shut behind the Speed King and left him in darkness.

The chill would have hit him right away. Kingsley would have pulled his hood up and shivered, praying that the driver would stop at the next M&S store and let him out. Soon his teeth would've been chattering and he'd have been hugging himself to keep warm. Maybe he would start to hammer on the partition between himself

and the cab. Or maybe frostbite would
set in.

When that happened, your fingers and
toes were the first things to go numb, and
probably your ears. After that, your whole
body froze up and you began to feel sleepy.
Your head started to nod, and you dreamed
weird things, like the fact that you were
sitting toasty and warm in front of a fire,
when really you were freezing to death in
the back of a lorry...

After that, curtains!

'Let's ring the police!' Tom gasped.

'No, wait!' Wayne held him back. 'I've
got a better idea!'

'Leggo! We gotta get Kingsley out of that
lorry fast!'

'That's what I've been trying to tell you!'
Wayne hung on and dragged Tom back
towards the main entrance into Marks and
Spencer. 'But forget the police; they'd take
too long. What we have to do is find out
exactly which lorry was in the bay that

Kingsley skated into. Then they can call the driver and tell him to stop and let him out!'

'Go over that one more time!' The man behind the desk in the M&S office fixed his silver-rimmed glasses more firmly on his nose. He studied Tom and Wayne closely as they went over their story a second time.

'Our friend's skateboard got out of control,' Wayne explained as carefully as he could, his face serious and his body leaning forward over the wide desk towards the man in the grey suit. 'He forgot to push down on his kicktail and he went flying through the air.'

'I see.' The manager didn't blink. 'Go on.'

'He couldn't stop himself, see. So his deck ran away with him across the square with the fountain, straight into the shopping centre!'

'A runaway skateboard; hmmm!'

This wasn't going well, Tom felt. Wayne

was taking ages to get to the point and The Suit was looking at his watch.

'Kingsley's a bit mad really,' he cut in. 'He probably could've stopped any time he liked, but skating through the shop was his idea of a joke!'

'A joke!' The Suit echoed.

Wayne took up the tale again. 'Only, when he shot through the delivery doors he wouldn't have been expecting the loading bay. He would've had to ollie over the edge into it. It was his bad luck that the frozen-food truck was there waiting.'

'It was like this!' Tom jumped up to demonstrate. Balancing on his board, he mimed jumping with his deck into a deep well, landing on a ramp and skating up into the truck.

'I see.' The manager made a tent-shape with his fingers.

'That was ages ago,' Wayne pointed out. 'Kingsley's locked up in a freezing lorry. He could be anywhere!'

'Yeah. We have to show you which bay, then you can call the driver and let Kingsley out!' Pausing for breath, Tom saw that the man had no intention of moving. 'What're you waiting for? C'mon, Kingsley could turn into a block of ice while we sit here explaining!'

Quietly the manager pressed a button on his phone.

Phew, at last! Tom and Wayne breathed a sigh.

'The case of the runaway skateboard! I take it you saw your–er–little friend land on the lorry ramp?'

'Kingsley's not little. He's the tallest kid in the class,' Wayne informed the manager.

Just make the call! Tom thought. *Do it!*

'We have to save him!' Wayne insisted.

The door opened and a man they'd seen before marched in. It was the tall security guard from the delivery area complete with flat peaked hat and a neat grey moustache.

'Please!' Wayne's voice rose to a squeak.

'What're we waiting for? Kingsley's gonna
die if we don't open that door!'

'What happened?' Wayne sagged against
a bike stand in Fountain Square. The Town
Hall clock struck one o'clock.

'They didn't believe us!' Tom stormed.
Stupid Suits, Dumb Uniforms! 'They kicked
us out!'

'Mr Stonehouse, I understand you've had
dealings with these two lads before?' The
Suit had said in his smooth snidey voice.

'Yessir!' the security guard had confirmed.
'They're the ones who snuck into the
delivery area and used it as an illegal
skateboarding park!'

'We didn't!'

'We were looking for Kingsley.'

'Quiet!' Snobby Suit had ordered. 'Did
you see a third boy?' he asked The Uniform.

'Description?' the guard had quizzed.

'Tall kid in a black hoodie with a skull on
the front and a red bandanna round his

head.' Tom had tried to deliver the answer.

'Nope.' Uniform had shaken his head.
'There was just the two, as far as I know.'

'And had a frozen-food container left
the depot in the few minutes before you
spotted them?' Suit had made a thorough
investigation.

'No Sir!'

'Sure?'

'Yessir!'

'Throw them out,' Suit had decided.

'B-b-but!'

'Hang on just a minute!'

'Now,' the manager had insisted. 'Before they waste any more of our time!'

So now Tom and Wayne stood by the fountain full of gloom and doom about poor Kingsley.

'They're so dumb!' Wayne moaned. 'Why would we make it up?'

'Dunno.' Tom was troubled:

a) He'd led Wayne astray.

b) They were both late for lunch.

c) They'd almost been arrested. In fact, if they'd held out for another second in the store manager's office, the cops would've been there, Tom was sure.

d) Kingsley was still missing. That added up to one seriously bad day.

'Even if he didn't skateboard into a frozen-food lorry,' Wayne conceded; 'even if it was only an ordinary lorry with pyjamas and slippers, they still should've got him back!'

Tom sat down on the low wall at the edge of the fountain. Bummer; Kingsley had really done it this time!

'He might be suffocating!' Wayne wailed. 'Or starving!'

'Yeah,' Tom agreed grimly. 'Or going stark, staring mad!'

Seven

Rrrrrr-clunk-swoop!

'Wha'ssat!' Tom yelped. He spun round, his back to the fountain.

RRRRRR-CLUNK-SWOOSH! A tall kid on a skateboard sped down the library ramp.

'KINGSLEY!' Tom and Wayne yelled.

Their mate stayed totally cool and perfectly balanced, weaving between pedestrians, plugged into his music and gently grooving. RRRRRRRRR-clickety click over the flagstones–NEEYAH! Kingsley sailed straight at Tom.

'What? How? Stop!' Tom put his hand up and stepped backwards.

Sploosh straight into the fountain!

Tom sat down hard in half a metre of clear, cold water. The shower from the fountain soaked him from head to foot. His precious skateboard floated out of his reach.

'Hah!' Kingsley bailed neatly. 'Got ya!'

Gulp! Swallowing water, scrambling after his deck, Tom went on his hands and knees under a torrent of water which spouted from the mouth of a giant marble fish. His baggy trousers ballooned out and threatened to slip off over his hips.

Tom made a grab for his belt. He clutched his trousers and sank down into the swirling pond, spewing water like the stone dolphin towering over him.

'Moonie! Moonie!' Kingsley crowed.

Tom felt savage. But he had to hang on to his trousers and grab his board. He splooshed some more, lunged and rescued the deck. Then he staggered out on to dry land.

'Tom's a trout!' Kingsley laughed, stooping to splash Wayne.

'Watch it!' A snooty woman passer-by threw Tom an accusing glance.

He snarled back.

'How did you get out of the lorry?' Wayne asked Kingsley in a high, astonished voice.

'What lorry?'

'The frozen-food lorry!'

Kingsley shrugged the question off. 'Dunno what you're on about.' He was still too busy laughing at Tom to pay much attention.

Splish-splash! Tom lifted his legs and shook water out of his trousers, then out of his hoodie. He took off his cap and used it to wipe his face.

'The frozen-food lorry that was parked there when you ollied off the platform!' Kingsley piped.

'Oh yeah, that lorry!' Kingsley grinned from ear to ear. 'The one I heard you and Tom rabbiting on about when I was hiding behind the concrete pillar in the delivery bay!'

'There's no lorry. There never was any lorry,

and there never will be!' Tom spelled it out for Wayne. 'This has all been Kingsley's idea of a big joke!!!'

'Yeah, and it worked!' Kingsley was back on his board, coasting around the outside of the fountain. Tom was still dripping, and Wayne was gawping and shaking his head. 'I just nipped behind the pillar and heard every word you said! *"Maybe there was a lorry here in this bay when Kingsley shot through the door!"'* He mimicked Wayne's worried voice, then Tom's frantic suggestion: *'"He could be on his way to the motorway, right now, this very minute!"'*

'You...sneaky snake!' Wayne chose his worst insult.

'Woooo-oooh!' Kingsley pretended to be scared. 'Hissss-save me!'

So Tom stepped across his path and made him bail. 'THIS IS NOT FUNNY!' he yelled.

Kingsley bent forward, clutched his stomach and laughed like a hyena.

'You watched us go to see Manager Four Eyes and get thrown out of his office!' Tom screeched. 'You let it happen!'

'Keep the noise down, lads.' A *Big Issue* seller came up to them and grumbled. 'Punters are avoiding my pitch because of you three.'

Tears of laughter rolled down Kingsley's cheeks. '"He could be on his way to the motorway...!"'

Right! Tom couldn't hold back any longer. He lunged at Kingsley, missed and sprawled on the floor.

'Lads, lads!' The magazine seller helped pick Tom up. He was small and thin, with two days' stubble and a blue and white striped woolly hat. 'Let's kiss and make up, shall we?'

'He wrecked my skateboard!' Tom accused wildly, holding up the dripping deck. 'Look, all the laminate's curling off!'

'Who, me?' Kingsley put on an innocent look and spread the palms of his hands upwards. 'What did I do?'

'No lorry?' Wayne was still muttering to himself.

'Right, beat it!' The *Big Issue* man had run out of patience. 'Go skate in the park where you won't bother anyone.'

Muttering, sighing and grinning, Tom, Wayne and Kingsley did as they were told.

'He wrecked my deck!' Tom scowled.

'No lorry?' Wayne was trying to get the facts straight.

'I pulled one cool trick on you, huh!' Swaggering on ahead, Kingsley bumped into Sasha Jones and Bex Stevens, who had just jumped off a bus. 'Hey, listen to this!' And he launched into the story of what had happened.

But Bex pushed him aside with one flick of her silky, light-brown hair. 'Shut up, Kingsley. No one's interested. Sasha and me came to find Tom.'

Hearing his name, Tom stopped fuming and tuned in.

'They came to find you-ooo, To-om!'
Kingsley sang, joking his way into
Jubilee Park.

'Shurrup, Kingsley!' Sasha warned. 'Keep
quiet and listen for once, why don't you!'

'Tom, we've got a message for you from
your mum.'

He stiffened. 'When did you see her?
What did she say?'

'She says, how come you're two hours late for lunch and why did you break your promise about looking after Wayne?' Sasha told him.

Tom's heart thudded.

'We saw her while we were waiting at the bus stop,' Bex explained in a clear, sensible voice. 'She asked us if we'd seen you at Jubilee Park this morning...'

'...And we said no,' Sasha added. She saw it as her job to finish other people's sentences for them. 'But we said that was where we were going now.'

It was Bex's turn to tut and interrupt. 'And your mum said if we saw you and Wayne, could we pass on a message?'

Tom and Wayne looked from Bex to Sasha, and back again. Tom's heart hadn't got back to normal after the massive thud. It was still twittering away inside his chest like a shed full of budgies. Was he in TROUBLE!

Bex narrowed her eyes and stared

sideways at him. 'I don't know what you've done, but it must be something serious!'

'What did Mum say?' he gasped.

This was worse than facing Waymann, worse even than torture!

'She said, stay where you are, she's coming to fetch you!' Sasha shot in. There, she'd delivered the message first and was enjoying its effect on Tom!

He felt his mouth go dry and his knees begin to shake. Not that he was scared of his mum; of course not.

Like, no way, dude!

No, the reason he was trembling was because of the Tom-how-could-you treatment he knew he would get.

He could cope with the dark look and the sharp go-to-your-room! No problem. He would slob upstairs, choose a skateboarding vid and watch it. By the time it was over, his mum would've forgotten that she'd ever told him off.

But the how-could-you stuff was horrible.

It was a shake of the head and a sigh. Then a long silence for Tom to understand how badly he'd let her down. After that, his dad would be brought in. That was even worse. Tom would feel like a worm, or a woodlouse. He would want to crawl away under a stone.

'Looks like you're for it,' Bex commented. She was the type who never got told off because she'd been grown-up since the moment she was born. She got stars and merits, badges on her blue school sweater and shiny shoes with pointy toes.

Tom sniffed. 'Don't care!' he lied.

'She's gonna fetch Wayne's mum with her,' Sasha announced. 'You're gonna get killed, both of you!'

'It's all your fault, Tom,' Bex decided. 'Wayne would never have been late if it hadn't been for you.'

'Me!' He made a feeble protest, but he knew she was right. Wayne had wanted to go home on time in case his mum worried.

'No, it's not.' Wayne stuck up for Tom. 'I invited him. We were well into skating and we forgot the time!'

'Tell that to the birds!' Sasha scoffed.

Yeah, dude! Tell that to the birds!

'Anyway, how come you got wet?' Bex quizzed Tom.

'He went for a swim in the fountain,' Kingsley laughed, skating along as if what had happened had nothing to do with him. He pulled a grind along a kerb, then ollied a flower bed.

'He's good!' Sasha admitted. She made out she didn't like to be impressed by a mere boy, but Kingsley was definitely the main man.

'Sasha fancies Kingsley,' Bex confided to Wayne. 'But

it won't last. Two weeks ago, she fancied Ryan. Next week it could even be you, Wayne.'

Wayne blushed beetroot-red.

Meanwhile, Kingsley pushed his envelope by heading for the new bandstand and working out which rad move he could pull. Tom blocked his ears and shut his eyes. He had to concentrate. Here, in the middle of the park, waiting for his mum and Jo Penny to land, he and Wayne didn't have many choices.

'What're you gonna do?' Sasha challenged.

'Run away!' Tom answered quickly.

'Where to?' As usual, Wayne was ready to follow Tom's lead.

'Yeah, where to?' Bex and Sasha joined in. Silence.

'Admit it, Tom, you've got nowhere to run!' Bex insisted.

'OK, then. We'll make up a mega lie!'

'Like what?' Sasha asked.

'Like, we were late because we helped an old lady cross the road, and it turned out she was blind, so we had to take her all the way home, and she lived on the other side of town and she didn't have any bus fare, so we gave her our own bus money, which meant we couldn't catch our bus home...'

Sasha and Bex stared and shook their heads.

'Don't even think about it,' Bex said.

'OK then, we'll stick with the truth for once!' Tom announced.

But when he'd gone through the runaway skateboard part, and the Marks and Spencer part, plus the bit about the invisible frozen-food lorry, Chippie chirped up. *No one will buy that story, dude!*

But it's the truth!

Forget it. They'll lock you up and throw away the key.

'Uh-oh, here come your mums!' Sasha announced. She pointed towards the gate.

Tom swallowed and turned slowly.

Yes, here they came; Jo Penny and his own mother storming along the path between the flowerbeds, sleeves rolled up and sternly fixing them with their eyes.

'Thomas!' Beth cried. 'Stay where you are. I want to know exactly what's been going on!'

Eight

Da-dum, da-dum, da-dum! Beth Bean and
Jo Penny came at a cavalry charge down
the park footpath.

'Let's hide!' Wayne cried.

'Run!' Sasha had changed her mind.

'No point,' Bex insisted calmly. 'They'll get
you in the end.'

Tom quaked in his trainers. His mum was
on the warpath. She'd been dragged into

town, away from her Saturday afternoon
stuff–shopping, gardening, chatting over a
cup of coffee–to deal with her monster-
child; the one who couldn't stay out of
trouble to save his life. Da-dum, da-dum!
She pounded towards him with that Tom-
how-could-you glare.

'Wayne!' Jo Penny was the first to speak.
'What happened? Are you all right?'

Wayne wriggled out of her anxious grasp.
'Yeah, Mum. I'm OK.' He ran on the spot
and waved his arms around. 'Look,
nothing's hurt!'

'You must be starving!' Jo wailed. 'You
haven't had any lunch!'

'Never mind lunch!' Beth stormed. 'Tom
Bean, what was the last thing I said to you
before you left?'

'Don't lead Wayne astray,' he mumbled.
Somehow, all the excuses had melted away,
leaving an empty space inside his head.
Mega bad dream. Double-double-double
nightmare.

'Exactly! And look what happens! I can't
trust you an inch, Tom. Poor Jo has been
worried out of her mind.'

'Sorry,' he muttered. Out of the corner
of one eye, he saw Sasha and Bex enjoying
the show. Behind them, loud-mouth
Kingsley was swooping around the
bandstand, plugged in and grooving.

'It was my fault!' Wayne insisted. 'I

wouldn't let Tom go home, honest!'

Beth and Jo considered this excuse, glanced at Wayne's flushed face, then shook their heads.

'That's very nice of you, Wayne,' Beth said kindly. 'But this bears all the hallmarks of one of Tom's typical escapades!'

Bex and Sasha smirked. Kingsley whirred and clunked.

'What're you gonna do?' Tom asked glumly.

Don't even ask, dude! Chippie would've squawked.

'First, I want you to apologise properly to Jo. After that I'm taking you home in the car.'

'Then what?' Tom wanted to know the worst.

'Then I take this board and I chop it up for firewood,' his mum said grimly, wrenching Tom's precious deck from his grasp. 'That's the end of your skateboarding career, Tom. From now on, you'll have to find something else to fill up your time.'

'Help!'

Don't look at me, dude. You're on your own.

'Do something! They can't do this! It's not fair!'

They're the ones pulling the strings here. Your dad feeds me. What can I say?

'Help, someone!'

No can do. Sorry, dude.

'No more skateboarding?' Tom's voice came out weak and strained. This was the end of life as he knew it. No skateboarding-he might as well give up and die!

'That's right.' Beth wasn't about to weaken, even though Tom's face had turned pale. 'If it's the only way of teaching you a lesson, that's how it has to be.'

'Perhaps that's a bit over the top,' Jo put in. 'After all, neither of them came to any harm.'

'No thanks to Tom,' Beth insisted. She held on tight to the board.

Behind them, Kingsley whizzed one last time around the wooden floor of the bandstand. He was doing over 20mph in a tight circle, getting ready to pull a rad big air exit down to the ground.

'Neeyah!' he cried, waving at all the dogs and picnickers, ignoring warnings to slow down and take care.

Woof! A red setter loped up into the bandstand to join Kingsley, followed by a black and white spaniel. Their owners soon came running, but they stopped on the grass, watching helplessly as their dogs and the skater whirled around.

Woof-yap-woof! The dogs raced and bounded in a brown, black and white blur.

Wheee! Kingsley swerved in and out.

'Stop it, Kingsley; I feel dizzy!' Sasha cried.

'What a show-off!' Bex tutted.

'Here, Wilf, here, boy!' the

spaniel's owner called in vain

Wooo-ooof! The setter pounced up
against Kingsley, knocking him clean off
his board.

Tom saw the loose deck shoot out under
the low railing, straight for the back of his
mum's head. He saw Kingsley stagger
backwards towards the bandstand steps
under the blur of fur.

'Watch it!' In a split second, Tom had rugby tackled his mum and sat her down on the grass while Kingsley's deck frisbeed into the park. It smacked into a lamppost, and fell safely to the ground.

'Woah!' Swamped by dogs, Kingsley roared and toppled. He fell backwards down four metal steps–bounce-bounce–hit the grass, rolled and lay there moaning.

'What happened?' Beth asked.

'Kingsley almost knocked your head off with his board,' Bex explained, calmly helping her to her feet. 'He's mega dangerous when he's showing off. But Tom saved you.'

'Call an ambulance! Somebody dial 999!' Jo Penny cried, seeing Kingsley lying on the grass with his eyes tight shut.

Tom took off his hoodie and ran to Kingsley.

First aid; rule number one: don't move the injured skater if they're unconscious or appear to be in severe pain. Keep them warm.

'Grab your dogs,' Tom told the two owners, making space around Kingsley and placing his hoodie over his chest.

'Stand back, everyone. Kingsley, can you hear me?'

Kingsley opened one eye and looked at Tom.

'Right. Can you move?'

'Uh.' He opened the other eye and turned his head.

'Call the ambulance!' Jo Penny insisted.

'Uh-uh!' Kingsley sat up holding his ribs. His red bandanna was crooked over one eye, both elbows were grazed, but he could stand and show everyone that he was OK.

'Trust Kingsley!' Bex tutted.

'Leave him alone,' Sasha insisted, pushing through to stand beside him. 'He can't help it if he's a total nutcase!'

'He ought to come with a warning,' Wilf's disgruntled owner muttered. 'Danger: Skaters damage your health!'

Gradually the noise had died down and the park was returning to normal. No broken bones, no blood. No need even for an ambulance. The picnickers went back to their crisps and egg sandwiches.

'You OK?' Tom double-checked.

Kingsley nodded, while Wayne went to fetch his board. For the first time, Kingsley noticed that Jo Penny and Tom's mum had arrived on the scene. 'Uh-oh; bad news?' he muttered to Tom.

Tom nodded. 'I'm banned,' he admitted.

'Hey, dude.' Kingsley shook his head and straightened his bandanna. 'Because of this morning?'

Tom nodded. He had to keep the tears out of his eyes, so he stooped for his hoodie and struggled back into it.

'That sucks,' Kingsley decided. Then, as if he suddenly saw the light, he asked, 'Hey man, did I drop you in it?'

'You could say that,' Tom admitted.

'Of course you did!' Bex had been

listening to every muttered word. 'Kingsley, it's totally down to you that Tom's banned!'

'So why help me just then?' Kingsley frowned. He still didn't get it.

Tom shrugged. 'You're part of the crew.' A crew that he couldn't belong to any more, worse luck.

'Is that it?' Kingsley asked, with a thoughtful tilt of his head.

'Yeah, and you're a mate,' Tom added. Whatever; through thick and thin, that never changed.

'Wait here,' Kingsley told him, marching across to Beth. He took a deep breath and gave it to her straight. 'Mrs Bean, you can't take away Tom's board and ban him from skating. He didn't do anything wrong.'

Tom, Wayne, Bex and Sasha stood in a huddle, jaws dropping, not believing what they were hearing; Kingsley actually holding his hand up to something for once in his life.

'I mean, that's never happened before!'

Bex whispered. 'Kingsley is Teflon Man-nothing ever sticks!'

'Sshh!' Sasha muttered. 'Listen!'

'Library ramp-Marshway Shopping Centre-Marks and Spencer...' Kingsley was telling Beth and Jo. 'I hid behind a pillar-Tom-motorway-frozen food!'

'I see!' Beth murmured. She looked from Kingsley to Tom and back again.

'And about the police earlier in the week...' Kingsley went on. 'Tom wasn't even there when we woke that baby up. He was miles away, across the other side of the park. That was me then, as well.'

'Really?' Beth was definitely seeing things in a new light. 'Is there anything else you'd like to say, Kingsley?'

'Yeah, Tom's a good dude. He takes care of Wayne. He never grassed me up.'

'Wow!' Sasha breathed. Kingsley was fessing up big style.

'I'm sorry.' Kingsley ended his big speech. 'And I think you should give Tom his board back. I mean, you can't take it away; the dude loves to skate!'

'So she didn't, and I can,' Tom told Wayne next morning in Hammett Park. He wore his cap, his shades and the long belt he'd nicked from his dad's drawer.

'She didn't take your board away?' Wayne echoed. 'And she'll let you skate?'

Tom nodded happily. They studied Kingsley perfecting his fakie tailstall, closely watched by Sasha and Bex. 'Cool, huh?'

'Yeah, cool,' Wayne agreed. After a pause he added, 'Anyway, I reckon your fakie tailstall is better than Kingsley's.'

Tom grinned, ready to skate down the hill. But Sasha ran up

to him with an important message.

'Bex Stevens wants to go out with you!' she whispered, loud enough for the whole park to hear.

Tom gulped and jumped on his board. No way! He needed a girlfriend like he needed a hole in the head. 'Kingsley!' he yelled at the top of his voice. He skated past Baldy-head pushing a pushchair. The baby squawked. Bex smiled at him as he sped by.

Tom looked the other way. 'Kingsley, wait for me,' he cried above the roar of his trucks. 'I want to show you a crazy new jump. Watch this, it's well sick!'

Tell the Me Truth, Tom!

Jenny Oldfield

Tom eyeballs a fox in Bernie King's
basement, but no one believes him. 'No way!
Dream on, Tom!' say his friends. Tom
decides to prove it. He's going to take a
picture of the fox...After all, the camera
never lies...Does it?

Watch Out, Wayne

Jenny Oldfield

Life's tough for Tom. He offers to be best
mates with new boy, Wayne, but it only lands
him in trouble—again! OK, maybe giving
Wayne a CRASH course in skateboarding
wasn't so smart.
But Tom meant well. Honest!

Get Lost, Lola

Jenny Oldfield

Tom is TOTALLY disgusted. Lola–aka, Little Miss Superglue–says she fancies him. Ergh! And Lola knows a shameful secret about Tom. If he doesn't agree to be her boyfriend, then the whole school will know it, too...Uh-oh! But would Lola really be that devious and mean?

Drop Dead, Danielle

Jenny Oldfield

Mean and mardy 'dob-them-in' Danielle is on Tom's case again–accusing him of flooding the school cloakroom! *As if.* Danielle says she's going to tell on Tom–and she probably will! Tom needs to prove it wasn't him–but how?

Don't Make Me Laugh, Liam

Jenny Oldfield

Tom's cousin Liam is coming over from
Dublin. Wicked! Liam is just like Tom—only ten
times noisier, and even more of a joker—he'll
probably give him a few handy tips! Uh-oh.
As if Tom really needs any encouragement...

TRADITIONAL
FOLKSONGS & BALLADS OF
SCOTLAND

40 COMPLETE SONGS, ARRANGED AND EDITED BY
John Loesberg

Volume One

OSSIAN

CONTENTS

Introduction

For most ageing folkies, like myself, the 60's were a major musical turning-point. The mixing of contemporary songs with a convincing restating of the old traditions was an immediate success, even with people who normally would stay well away from anything like folk music.

The efforts of individuals, like Ewan MacColl, Jeannie Robertson, groups like The Battlefield Band, Gaberlunzie, Boys of the Lough, Corries, MacCalman's, and the singing families such as the Campbells of Aberdeen, the Fishers and the Stewarts of Blair showed us that all these strange old songs which our grandparents were just about beginning to forget were a vast treasure which quickly took on a new lease of life.

Here was an astounding human heritage of stories about the lives of ordinary folk, but also of heroes, despots, sailors and beggar-kings. As if the stories were not enough in themselves, the tunes in which the words were wrapped were also of a rare beauty.

Here then are some of the songs of a people for whom music making has always been a serious and all-embracing occupation.
The sheer volume, variety and quality of the entire corpus of Scots balladry made it very hard indeed to make a reasonable selection. I aimed at getting a good cross-section of all main types of Scots songs — from the great Child ballads, love, work and historical songs, to children's ditties and down to earthy bothy ballads.

Some songs which are not of a particularly venerable age or of obvious traditional origins such as 'The Auld Hoose' and others were included simply because I know singers are always looking for these old favourites.

Although keys, chords and even metronome setting have been indicated, it should be clear that as with all folk music, it is you, the singer, who will treat each song the way *you* prefer it. In any case - never feel shy to sing a song in a higher or lower register rather than strain the auld vocal chords !

Being afflicted as I am with a slight aversion against 7th chords, I have left them out of the arrangements as much as I could. I've always felt they're more suited to classical songs than to folk music.

I thank the many singers, libraries and institutions who helped me on my way and never hesitated to share with me the joy of Scottish Music.

John Loesberg
Aug 1993

'My definition of an intellectual is someone who can listen to the William Tell Overture without thinking of The Lone Ranger'

Billy Connolly

Cam Ye O'er Frae France ?

♩ = 138

Geordie he's a man, there is little doubt o't,
He's done a' he can, wha' can do without it ?
Down there came a blade, linkin like my lordie;
He wad drive a trade, at the loom o' Geordie.

Though the claith were bad, blithely may we niffer;
Gin we get a wab, it makes little differ.
We hae tint our plaid, bonnet, belt and swordie,
Ha's and mailins braid - but we hae a Geordie !

Jocky's gane to France, and Montgomery's lady;
There they'll learn to dance: Madam are you ready ?
They'll be back belyve, belted, brisk and lordly;
Brawly may they thrive, to dance a jig wi' Geordie !

Hey for Sandy Don !, Hey for Cockalorum !
Hey for Bobbing John, and his Highland quorum !
Mony a sword and lance, swings at Highland hurdie;
How they'll skelp and dance, o'er the bum o' Geordie !

OMB 93

MacPherson's Farewell

♩ = 96

It was by a woman's treacherous hand
That I was condemned to dee.
Below a ledge at a window she stood,
And a blanket she threw o'er me.

Chorus

The laird o' Grant, that Highland sant,
That first laid hands on me,
He played the cause on Peter Broon
To let MacPherson die.

Chorus

Untie these bands from off my hands
And gie to me my sword
An' there's no a man in all Scotland
But I'll brave him at a word.

Chorus

There's some come here to see me hanged,
And some to buy my fiddle
But before that I do part wi' her
I'll brak her thro' the middle.

Chorus

He took the fiddle into baith o' his hands,
And he broke it ower a stone.
Says: 'There's nae ither hand shall play on thee
When I am dead and gone.'

Chorus

O little did my mother think,
When first she cradled me
That I would turn a rovin' boy
And die on the gallows tree.

Chorus

The reprieve was comin' ower the brig o' Banff
To let MacPherson free;
But they pit the clock a quarter afore
And hanged him to the tree.

Chorus

OMB 93

Lang A-Growing

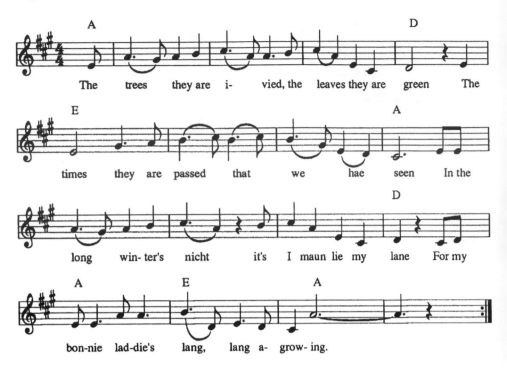

O, father, dear father, ye hae done me muckle wrang,
For ye hae wedded me to a lad that's ower young,
For he is but twelve and I am thirteen,
And my bonnie laddie's lang, lang a-growing.

O dochter, dear dochter, I hae done ye nae wrang,
For I hae wedded you to a noble laird's son
And he shall be the laird and you shall wait on,
And a' the time your lad'll be a-growing.

O, father, dear father, if you think it will fit,
We'll send him to the school for a year or twa yet,
And we'll tie a green ribbon around about his bonnet
And that'll be a token that he's married.

O, father, dear father, and if it pleases you
I'll cut my long hair abune my broo;
Vest, coat and breeks I will gladly put on,
And I to the school will gang wi' him.

She's made him a sark o' the holland so fine
And she has sewed it wi' her fingers ain;
And aye she loot the tears doon fa'
Crying, my bonnie laddie's lang, lang a-growing.

In his twelfth year, he was a married man,
And in his thirteenth he had gotten her a son;
And in his fourteenth, his grave it grew green
And that's put an end to his growing.

OMB 93

Ye Jacobites by name

Ye Ja - co - bites by name, Give an ear, give an ear, Ye

Ja - co - bites by name, give an ear; Ye

Ja - co - bites by name, your fautes I will pro - claim, Your

doc - trines I mun blame, You shall hear.

What is right and what is wrong, by the law, by the law ?
What is right and what is wrong, by the law ?
What is right and what is wrong, a short sword and a long,
A weak arm and a strong for to draw, for to draw,
A weak arm and a strong for to draw.

What makes heroic strife famed afar, famed afar ?
What makes heroic strife famed afar ?
What makes heroic strife, to whet the assassin's knife,
Or hunt a parent's life wi' bloody war, bloody war,
Or hunt a parent's life wi' bloody war ?

Then leave your schemes alone in the state, in the state,
Then leave your schemes alone in the state,
Then leave your schemes alone, adore the rising sun,
And leave a man alone to his fate, to his fate,
And leave a man alone to his fate.

Plooman Laddies

Doon yon-der den there's a ploo-man lad, An' sime
sim-mer's day he'll be a' my ain An' sing lad-die O, an' sing
lad-die aye The ploo-man lad- dies are a' the go

I love his teeth an' I love his skin —
I love the verra cairt he hurls in.

Chorus

Doon yonder den I coulda gotten a merchant,
But a' his stuff wisna worth a groat.

Chorus

Doon yonder den I coulda gotten a miller,
But the smell o' dust widda deen me ill.

Chorus

It's ilka time I gyang tae the stack,
I hear his whip gie an ither crack.

Chorus

I see him comin' frae yonder toon,
Wi' a' his ribbons hinging' roon an' roon.

Chorus

An' noo she's gotten her plooman lad,
As bare as ever he left the ploo.

Chorus

OMB 93

The Day we went to Rothesay, O

One Hog-ma-ny at Gles-ca Fair, There was me, my-sel' and
sev'- ral mair, We a' went off to hae a tear an'
spend the nicht in Rothe-say, O, We wan- dered thro' the
Broom- i- law, thro' wind an' rain an' sleet an' snaw, And at
for- ty mi- nutes af- ter twa, We got the length o'
Rothe -say -O, A- dir- rum- a doo a dum a day, a
dir- rum- a doo a dad- dy O A dir- rum- a doo a

dum   a   day,   The   day   we went   to   Rothe- say, O

A sodger lad named Ru'glen Will,
Wha's regiment's lyin' at Barra Hill,
Gaed off wi' a tanner to get a gill
In a public hoose in Rothesay-O.
Said he 'I think I'd like to sing'
Said I 'Ye'll no' dae sic a thing'
He said 'Clear the room and I'll mak' a ring
And I'll fecht them all in Rothesay, O.

Chorus

In search of lodgins we did slide,
To find a place where we could bide;
There was eighty-twa o' us inside
In a single room in Rothesay, O.
We a' lay doon to tak' our ease,
When somebody happened for to sneeze,
And he wakened half a million fleas
In a single room in Rothesay, O.

Chorus

There were several different kinds of bugs,
Some had feet like dyer's clogs,
And they sat on the bed and they cockit their lugs,
And cried 'Hurrah for Rothesay, O !
'O noo', says I, 'we'll have to 'lope'
So we went and joined the Band O'Hope,
But the polis wouldna let us stop
Another nicht in Rothesay, O.

Chorus

13

CMB 93

The Jolly Beggar

♩ = 88

There was a jol - ly beg - gar, and a- beg - gin' he was boun'; And

he took up his quar - ters in - to a land - wart toun, And we'll

gang nae mair a - rov - in', a - rov - in' in the night, And we'll

gang nae mair a - ro - vin', let the moon shine e'er sae bright, And we'll

gang nae mair a - ro - vin'.

He wad neither lie into the barn, nor yet wad he in byre,
But in ahint the ha' door, or else beyont the fire.

Chorus

The beggar's bed was made at e'en, wi guid clean straw and hay,
Just ahint the ha' door, and there the beggar lay.

Chorus

Up raise the guidman's dochter, and a' to bar the door,
And there she saw the beggar man was standin' on the floor.

Chorus

He took the lassie in his arms, and to the neuk he ran,
'O! hooly, hooly, wi' me sir, ye'll wauken our guidman.'

Chorus

He took his horn frae his side, and blew baith loud and shrill,
And four and twenty belted knights came skippin' o'er the hill.

Chorus

And he took out his little knife, loot a' his duddies fa',
And he stood the brawest gentleman that was amang them a'.

Chorus

OMB 93

I'll Lay Ye Doon, Love

I hae travelled faur frae Inverey,
Aye and as faur as Edinburgh toon,
But it's I must gae, love, and travel further,
And when I return, I will lay ye doon.

Chorus

I maun leave ye noo, love, but I'll return
Tae ye my love and I'll tak' your hand,
Then no more I'll roam frae ye my love,
No more tae walk on the foreign sand.

Chorus

Dumbarton's Drums

♩ = 84

Dum- bar- ton's drums they sound so bon-nie, And they remind me o' my John-nie, Such fond de- light doth steal upon me When John-nie kneels and kis-ses me.

Across the fields o' boundin' heather
Dumbarton tolls the hour of pleasure
A song of love that's without measure
When Johnnie sings his sangs tae me.

'Tis he alone that can delight me
His rovin' eye, it doth invite me,
And when his tender arms enfold me
The blackest night doth turn and flee.

My Johnnie is a handsome laddie
And though he is Dumbarton's caddie,
Some day I"ll be a captain's lady
When Johnnie tends his vows tae me.

OMB 93

Maggie Lauder

2 'Maggie,' quo' he, 'and by my bags,
 I'm fidgin' fain to see thee;
 Sit down by me my bonnie bird,
 In troth I winna steer thee.
 For I'm a piper to my trade,
 My name is Rob the Ranter;
 The lasses loup as they were daft
 When I blaw up my chanter.'

3 'Piper,' quo' Meg, 'hae you your bags ?
 Or is your drone in order ?
 If ye be Rob, I've heard of you,
 Live you upon the border ?
 The lasses a', baith far and near,
 Ha'e heard o' Rob the Ranter;
 I'll shake my foot wi' right guid will,
 Gif you'll blaw up your chanter.'

4 Then to his bags he flew wi' speed,
 About the drone he twistet;
 Meg up and wallop'd o'er the green,
 For brawly could she frisk it.
 'Weel done,' quo he — 'Play up,' quo' she,
 'Weel bobb'd,' quo Rob the Ranter.
 ''Tis worth my while to play indeed,
 When I ha'e sic a dancer.'

5 'Weel ha'e you play'd your part,' quo' Meg,
 'Your cheeks are like the crimson;
 There's nane in Scotland plays sae weel,
 Since we lost Habbie Simpson.
 I've lived in Fife, baith maid and wife,
 These ten years and a quarter;
 Gin ye should come to Anster fair,
 Spier ye for Maggie Lauder.'

Hieland Laddie

♩ = 80

Will ye go to In - ver - ness, Bon - nie lad - die,

Hie - land lad - die? There you'll see the Hie - land dress,

Bon - nie lad - die, Hie - land lad - die. Phil - a beg and

bon - net blue, Bon - nie lad - die, Hie - land lad - die,

For the lad that wears the trews,

Bon - nie lad - die, Hie - land lad - die.

Geordie sits in Charlie's chair,
Bonnie laddie, Hieland laddie,
Had I my will he'd no sit there,
Bonnie laddie, Hieland laddie.
Ne'er reflect on sorrows past,
Bonnie laddie, Hieland laddie;
Charlie will be King at last,
Bonnnie laddie, Hieland laddie.

Time and tide come round to a',
Bonnie laddie, Hieland laddie,
And upstart pride will get a fa',
Bonnie laddie, Hieland laddie,
Keep up your heart, for Charlie fight,
Bonnie laddie, Hieland laddie,
Come what may, ye've done what's right,
Bonnie laddie, Hieland laddie.

OMB 93

Loch Tay Boat Song

♩ = 104

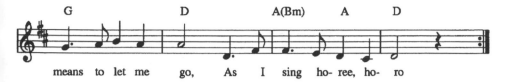

means to let me go, As I sing ho-ree, ho-ro

Nighean ruadh your lovely hair, has more glamour I declare,
Than all the tresses rare, 'tween Killin and Aberfeldy.
Be they lint white, brown or gold, be they blacker than the sloe,
They are worth no more to me, than the melting flake o' snow.
Her eyes are like the gleam, o' the sunlight on the stream,
And the song the fairies sing, seems like songs she sings at milking.
But my heart is full of woe, for last night she bade me go,
And the tears begin to flow, as I sing ho-ree, ho-ro.

The Wee, Wee German Lairdie

 = 92

An' he's clappit doun in our gudeman's chair,
The wee, wee German lairdie;
An' he's brocht fouth o' his foreign trash,
An' dibbled them in his yairdie.
He's pu'd the rose o' English loons,
An' broken the harp o' Irish clowns,
But our Scotch thistle will jag his thumbs,
This wee, wee German lairdie.

Come up amang our Hieland Hills,
Thou wee, wee German lairdie,
An' see the Stuart's lang kail thrive,
They hae dibbled in our kail-yairdie.
An' if a stock ye daur to pu',
Or haud the yokin' o' a plough,
We'll break your sceptre owre your mou',
Ye feckless German lairdie.

Auld Scotland, thou'rt ower cauld a hole,
For nursin' siccan vermin;
But the very dogs in England's court,
They bark an' howl in German.
Then keep thy dibble in thy ain hand,
Thy spade but an' thy yairdie;
For wha the deil now claims your land,
But a wee, wee German lairdie ?

OMB 93

The Bluebells of Scotland

♩ = 76

O, where tell me where, is your High - land lad - die gone? O
where, tell me where, is your High - land lad - die gone? 'He's
gone wi' stream - ing ban - ners, where nob - le deeds are done; And it's
oh! in my heart I wish him safe at home.

'O what, lassie, what does your Highland laddie wear ?
O what lassie, what does your Highland laddie wear ?'
'A Scarlet coat and bonnet wi' bonnie yellow hair,
And there's nane in the world can wi' my love compare.'

'O what will you claim for your constancy to him ?
O what will you claim for your constancy to him ?'
'I'll claim a priest to wed us, and a clerk to say 'Amen!'
And I'll ne'er part again from my bonnie Highlandman.'

The Reel of Stumpie-O

$\quad$ = 152

Hap and rowe, hap and rowe, hap and rowe, the
fee - tie o't; I thocht I was a maid - en fair,
Till I heard the gree - tie o't. My
dad - die was a fid - dler fine, My min - nie she made
man - kie O, and I my - self a thum - pin' quean, Wha
danced the reel of Stum - pie O.

Dance and sing, dance and sing,
Hey the merry dancing-O;
And a' their love-locks waving round,
And a' their bright eyes glancing-O.
The pipes come wi' their gladsome note
And then wi' dool and dumpie-O,
But the lightest tune to a maiden's foot
Is the gallant reel of Stumpie-O.

The gossip cup, the gossip cup,
The kimmer clash and caudle-O
The glowing moon, the wanton loon,
The cutty stool and cradle -O.
Douce dames maun hae their bairntime borne,
Sae dinna glower sae glumpie-O
Birds love the morn and craws love corn,
And maids the reel of Stumpie-O.

Repeat first verse

OMB 93

The Gaberlunzie Man

The nicht bein' dark and somewhat wat
Doun by the fireside the aul' man sat;
He cuist the mealpock aff his back
An' sae loudly he lilted an' sang
Ladlee a tow row ree

The lassie sat ayont the fire
An' aye she sang to his desire;
An' aye she sang to his desire,
'Would you lodge a leal puir man?'
Ladlee a tow row ree

'I'll bend my back an' bow my knee
An' tie a black patch owre my ee
An' for a beggar they'll tak me,
An' awa' wi' you I'll gang.
Ladlee a tow row ree

'Rise gudeman an' wauken your bairn
The cheese is to mak' an the claes to iron,
An' tell her to come speedily ben
For I'm sure she has lain owre lang.
Ladlee a tow row ree

Up i' the mornin' the auld man rase
He missed the beggar an' his auld claes,
He missed the beggar an' his auld claes,
'I hope there's nane o' oor gude gear gane.'
Ladlee a tow row ree

He ran to the cupboard, he ran to the kist
There was naething awa' that he could miss,
'Since a' thing's right then Praise be blest,
We lodged a leal puir man.'
Ladlee a tow row ree

Then he gaed to the bed where his dochter lay
The sheets were cauld an' she was away,
The sheets were cauld an' she was away,
Away wi' the beggar man.
Ladlee a tow row ree

When ten months were past and twelvemonth gane
The same beggar carle came again,
An' was askin' help for charitee
'Could you lodge a beggar man.'
Ladlee a tow row ree

'I never lodged a man but ane
I never had a dochter but ane,
An awa' wi' a beggar she has gane,
An' I dinna ken nor when nor where.'
Ladlee a tow row ree

'Yonder's your dochter comin' owre lea
An' mony a fine tale she'll tell thee,
She has got a bairn on ilka knee,
An' anither on the road comin' hame.'
Ladlee a tow row ree

27

Cauld Kail in Aberdeen

♩ = 80

There's cauld kail in A- ber- deen, And cas- tocks in Stra'-
bo - gie, Gin I hae but a bon - nie lass, Ye're wel -come to your
co - gie. And ye may sit up a' the night, And
drink till it be braid day -light; Gi'e me a lass baith clean and tight, To
dance the reel o' Bo - gie.

2 In cotillons the French excel,
   John Bull loves country dances;
   The Spaniards dance fandangoes well,
   Mynheer an all'mande prances.
   In foursome reels the Scots delight,
   At threesomes they dance wondrous light,
   But twasomes ding a' out o' sight,
   Danc'd to the reel o' Bogie.

3 Come lads, and view your partners weel
   Wale each a blythesome rogie;
   I'll tak' this lassie to mysel',
   She looks sae keen and vogie.
   Now piper lad, bang up the spring,
   The country fashion is the thing,
   To pree their mou's ere we begin
   To dance the reel o' Bogie.

4 Now ilka lad has got a lass,
   Save yon auld doited fogie,
   And ta'en a fling upon the grass,
   As they do in Stra'bogie.
   But a' the lasses look sae fain,
   We canna think oursel's to hain,
   For they maun hae their come again,
   To dance the reel o' Bogie.

5 Now a' the lads hae done their best,
   Like true men o' Stra'bogie,
   We'll stop a while and tak' a rest,
   And tipple out a cogie.
   Come now, my lads, and tak' your glass,
   And try ilk ither to surpass,
   In wishing health to ev'ry lass
   To dance the reel o' Bogie.

The Piper o' Dundee

♩ = 84

The pi-per cam' to our town, to our town, to our town, The pip-er cam' to our town, And he play'd bon-ni-lie. He play'd a spring, the laird to please, A spring brent new, frae 'yont the seas, And then he ga'e his bags a squeeze. And played an-i-ther key. And was-na he a ro-gie, A ro-gie, a ro-gie; And was-na he a ro-gie, The pi-per o' Dun-dee.

He played 'The welcome o'er the main',
And 'Ye'se be fou, and I'se be fain',
And 'Auld Stuart's back again'
Wi' muckle mirth and glee.
He play'd 'The Kirk', he play'd 'The Queer',
'The Mullin Dhu', and 'Chevalier',
And 'Lang away, but welcome here',
Sae sweet, sae bonnily.
And wasna he etc.

It's some gat swords, and some gat nane,
And some were dancing mad their lane;
And mony a vow o' weir was ta'en,
That night at Amulrie.
There was Tullibardine and Burleigh,
And Struan, Keith and Ogilvie;
And brave Carnegie, wha but he,
The piper o' Dundee ?
And wasna he etc.

OMB 93

The Calton Weaver

♩ = 69

As I cam' in by Glesca city,
Nancy Whisky I chanced to smell,
So I gaed in, sat doon beside her,
Seven lang years since I lo'ed her well.

Chorus

The mair I kissed her, the mair I lo'ed her,
The mair I kissed her, the mair she smiled,
Soon I forgot my mither's teaching,
Nancy soon had me beguiled.

Chorus

I woke up early in the morning,
To slake my drouth it was my need;
I tried to rise but I wasna able,
For Nancy had me by the heid.

Chorus

'Tell me landlady, whit's the lawin'?
Tell me whit there is to pay.'
'Fifteen shillings is the reckoning,
Pay me quickly and go away.'

Chorus

As I went oot by Glesca city
Nancy Whisky I chanced to smell;
I gaed in, drank four and sixpence
A' 'twas left was a crooked scale.

Chorus

I'll gang back to the Calton weaving
I'll surely mak' the shuttles fly
For I'll mak' mair at the Calton weaving
Than ever I did in a roving way.

Chorus

Come all ye weavers, Calton weavers,
A' ye weavers, where e'er ye be;
Beware of whisky, Nancy whisky,
She'll ruin you as she ruined me.

Chorus

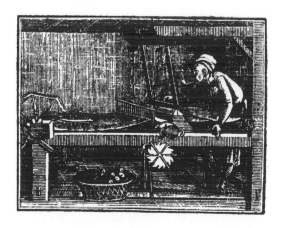

OMB 93

O Can Ye Sew Cushions ?

♩ = 108

I biggit the cradle upon the treetop,
And aye as the wind blew, my cradle did rock.
And hush a baw baby, O ba lil li loo,
And hee and baw, birdie, my bonnie wee doo.

Chorus

Now hush a baw lammie, and hush a baw dear,
Now hush a baw lammie, thy minnie is here.
The wild wind is ravin', thy minnie's heart sair,
The wild wind is ravin', but ye dinna care.

Chorus

Sing bal la loo lammie, sing bal la loo dear,
Does wee lammie ken that its daddie's no here ?
Ye're rockin' fu' sweetly on mammie's warm knee,
But daddie's a rockin' upon the saut sea.

Chorus

Annie Laurie

Her brow is like the snawdrift, her neck is like the swan,
Her face it is the fairest, that e'er the sun shone on;
That e'er the sun shone on, and dark blue is her e'e,
And for bonnie Annie Laurie, I'd lay me doun and dee.

Like dew on the gowan lying, is the fa' o' her fairy feet;
And like winds in summer sighing, her voice is low and sweet;
Her voice is low and sweet, she's a' the world to me,
And for bonnie Annie Laurie, I'd lay me doun and dee.

A Man's A Man For A' That

♩ = 76

Is there for ho- nest po- ver- ty, That hangs his head, an' a' that, The
co- ward slave, we pass him by; We dare be poor for a' that. For
a' that, an' a' that, Our toils ob- scure, and a' that, The
rank is but the gui- nea stamp; The man's the gowd for a' that.

2 What though on hamely fare we dine,
  Wear hoddin grey, an a' that ?
  Gie fools their silks, and knaves their wine,
  A man's a man for a' that.
  For a' that, an' a' that,
  Their tinsel show, an' a' that,
  The honest man, tho' e'er sae poor,
  Is king o' men for a' that.

3 Ye see yon birkie ca'd a lord,
  Wha struts, an' stares, an' a' that;
  Tho' hundreds worship at his word,
  He's but a coof for a' that.
  For a' that, an' a' that,
  His ribband, star, an' a' that,
  The man of independent mind
  He looks an' laughs at a' that.

4 A prince can mak a belted knight,
  A marquis, duke, an' a' that;
  But an honest man's aboon his might,
  Gude faith, he maunna fa' that !
  For a' that, an' a' that,
  Their dignities an' a' that,
  The pith o' sense, an' pride o' worth,
  Are higher rank than a' that.

5 Then let us pray that come it may,
  (As come it will for a' that)
  That Sense and Worth, o'er a' the earth,
  Shall bear the gree, an' a' that.
  For a' that, an' a' that,
  It's coming yet for a' that,
  That man to man, the world o'er,
  Shall brithers be for a' that.

CMB 93

The Bonnie Lass O' Fyvie O

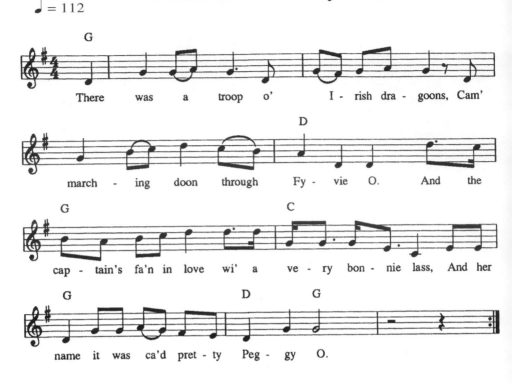

O come doon the stair, pretty Peggy, my dear
O come doon the stair pretty Peggy O
O come doon the stair and comb back your yellow hair
Tak a last fareweel o' your Daddie O.

'What way could I come doon, when I'm locked into a room
What way could I come doon' she said so saucy O
What way could I come doon, when I'm locked into a room
And a well dug below my window O.'

It's I'll gie ye ribbons love, and I'll gie you rings
I'll gie you a necklace o' amber O,
I'll gie ye silken petticoats wi' flounces to the knee,
Gin ye'll convoy me doon to my chamber O.'

What would your minnie think if she heard the guineas clink
What would your minnie think pretty Peggy O ?
What would your minnie think if she heard the guineas clink
And the hautboys playing afore ye O ?

O little would she think though she heard the guineas clink
O little would she think of her daughter O,
O little would she think though she heard the guineas clink
If I went and followed a sodger O.

It's braw, ay it's braw a captain's wife to be,
It's braw to be a captain's lady O,
It's braw to rise and rant and to follow with the camp,
And to march when your captain he is ready O.

A sodger's wife I never shall be
A sodger shall never enjoy me O
I never do intend to gang to a foreign land
I never will marry a sodger O.

The colonel cries: 'Boys mount boys mount'
But the captain cries: 'Tarry O,
O tarry for a while, just another day or twa,
Just to see if the bonnie lass will marry O.'

But up then spoke his brother John
And oh but he spoke sae saucy O
Says: 'What needs ye sae sorry be
There's mony a bonnie lassie afore ye O.'

I'll drink nae mair o' your guid claret wine
I'll drink nae mair o' your glasses O
For the morn is the day that I maun march away
So adieu to all you Fyvie lasses O.

So the drums they did beat by the bonnie Bogs o' Gight
And the band played by the lowlands o' Fyvie O
And aye as they played the captain he said:
'Bonnie lassie I'm gaun to leave ye O.'

But lang ere they won to bonnie Meldrum toon
They got their captain to carry O
And lang ere they won into bonnie Aberdeen
They got their captain to bury O.

So the drums they did beat and the fifes they did play
And the bands played the lowlands o' Fyvie O,
And the captain's name was Ned and he died for a maid
And he died for the chambermaid o' Fyvie O.

Green grow the birks upon bonnie Ytanside
And low lie the lowlands o' Fyvie O,
There's mony a bonnie lass in the howe o' Auchterless
But the flooer o' them a' lies in Fyvie O.

There's mony a bonnie lass in the Howe o' Auchterless
There's mony a bonnie lass in the Geerie O,
There's mony a bonnie Jean in the toon o' Aiberdeen
But the flooer o' them a' lies in Fyvie O.

OMB 93

Jockey's ta'en the Parting Kiss

♩ = 92

C   Dm   G7   C

Jock- ey's ta'en the part- ing kiss, O'er the moun-tains he is gane,

Am   Em   C   G7   C   G7   F   C G7 C

And with him is a' my bliss, Nought but griefs with me re- main.

Dm   G   Am   Dm   G   G7

Spare my Love, ye winds that blaw, Plash- y sleets and beat- ing rain !

C   F   G7   C   G7   C G7 C

Spare my Love, thou feath-'ry snaw, Drift- ing o'er the fro-zen plain !

When the shades of evening creep
O'er the day's fair, gladsome e'e,
Sound and safely may he sleep,
Sweetly blythe his waukening be.

He will think on her he loves,
Fondly he'll repeat her name;
For where'er he distant roves,
Jockey's heart is still at hame.

Charlie is my Darling

♩ = 92

O, Char - lie is my dar - ling, my dar - ling, my dar - ling! Char - lie is my dar - ling, The young Che - va - lier. 'Twas on a Mon - day mor - ning, Right ear - ly in the year, When Char - lie came to our town, The young Che - va - lier.

2 As he cam' marching up the street,
   The pipes played loud and clear,
   And a' the folks cam' rinnin' out,
   To meet the Chevalier.

   Chorus

3 Wi' Highland bonnets on their heads,
   And claymores bright and clear,
   They cam' to fight for Scotland's right,
   And the young Chevalier.

   Chorus

4 They've left their bonnie Hieland hills,
   Their wives and bairnies dear,
   To draw the sword for Scotland's lord,
   The gay Chevalier.

   Chorus

5 Oh, there were mony beating hearts,
   And mony hope and fear;
   And mony were the pray'rs put up
   For the young Chevalier.

   Chorus

OMB 93

Tae the Beggin' I Will Go

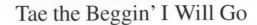

♩ = 92

O' a' the trades that man can try, The beg-gin' is the best, For when a man gets wea-ried he can aye sit doon an' rest, Tae the beg-gin' I will go, will go, Tae the beg-gin' I will go.

Before that I do gang awa', I'll lat my beard grow lang,
An' for my nails I winna pare, for beggars wears them lang.
Tae the begging I will go, will go, tae the begging I will go.

I'll gang to some greasy cook, an' buy an auld hat,
Wi' twa-three inches o' a rim, an' glittering o'er wi' fat,
Tae the begging I will go, will go, tae the begging I will go.

I'll gang and seek my quarters, afore that it grows dark,
Jist when the guidman comes, in frae his wark,
Tae the begging I will go, will go, tae the begging I will go.

Maybe the guidman will say: 'Puir man, come inby,
We'll a' sit close thegither, it's been a caul' day,'
Tae the begging I will go, will go, tae the begging I will go.

Then I'll take out my muckle dish, an' tramp it full o' meal —
Gin ye gie me bree, guidwife, I winna seek your kale,
Tae the begging I will go, will go, tae the begging I will go.

Maybe the guidwife will say: 'Keep in yer pickle meal,
Ye're welcome to yer quarters, likewise yer brose and kail,
Tae the begging I will go, will go, tae the begging I will go.

Gin a marriage ever chance, it happen to be here,
I will lay my blessing, on that happy pair,
Tae the begging I will go, will go, tae the begging I will go.

Some will gie me bread and beef, some will gie me cheese,
An' oot among the marriage folk, I'll gather the bawbees,
Tae the begging I will go, will go, tae the begging I will go.

Gin I come on as I do think, I'll come back and tell;
An' gin I dinna dae that, I'll keep it to mysel'.
Tae the begging I will go, will go, tae the begging I will go.

41

The Bonnie Earl o' Moray

Oh ! Wae betide ye, Huntly, and wherefore did ye sae ?
I bade ye bring him wi' you, and forbad' ye him to slay.
He was a braw gallant, and he played at the glove;
And the bonnie Earl o' Moray, he was the Queen's love.
Oh ! Lang will his ladye look frae the Castle Doune
Ere she see the Earl o' Moray come soundin' through the toun.

The Band o' Shearers

♩ = 112

Oh sum- mer days and heath- er bells come
bloom- ing owre yon high, high hills; There's yel- low corn in
a' the fields, And au- tumn brings the shear- in'

Chorus:
Bonnie lassie will ye gang
And shear wi' me the hale day lang?
And love will cheer us as we gang
Tae join yon band o' shearers.

Oh, if the weather be owre hot
I'll cast my cravat and my coat
And shear wi' ye amang the lot,
When we join yon band o' shearers.

And if the thistle is owre strang,
And pierce your lily milk-white hand,
It's wi' my hook I'll cut them down,
When we gang tae the shearin'.

And if the weather be owre dry,
They'll say there's love twixt you and I
We'll slyly pass each ither by,
When we join the band o' Shearers.

And when the shearin' it is done
And slowly sets the evening sun,
We'll have some rantin' roarin' fun,
And gang nae mair tae the shearin'.

Final Chorus:
So bonnie lassie bricht and fair
Will ye be mine for evermair?
If ye'll be mine, then I'll be thine,
And we gang nae mair tae the shearin'

OMB 93

The Auld Hoose

♩ = 66

Oh the auld hoose, the auld hoose, what tho' the rooms were wee, Oh
kind hearts were dwel - ling there, And bair - nies fu' o' glee. The
wild rose and the jes - sa - mine Still hang up - on the wa'. How
mo - ny cher - ish'd mem - o - ries Do they, sweet flow'rs, re - ca'.

Oh, the auld laird, the auld laird,
Sae canty, kind and crouse;
How mony did he welcome
To his ain wee dear auld hoose.
And the leddy too, sae genty,
There shelter'd Scotland's heir,
And clipt a lock wi' her ain hand
Frae his lang yellow hair.

The mavis still doth sweetly sing,
The blue bells sweetly blaw;
The bonnie Earn's clear windin' still,
But the auld hoose is awa'.
The auld hoose, the auld hoose,
Deserted tho' ye be,
There ne'er can be a new hoose
Will seem sae fair to me.

Still flourishin' the auld pear tree,
The bairnies liked to see;
And oh ! how aften did they spier
When ripe they a' wad be.
The voices sweet, the wee bit feet,
Aye rinnin' here and there;
The merry shout — oh! whiles we greet
To think we'll hear nae mair !

For they are a' wide scatter'd now,
Some to the Indies gane;
And ane alas ! to her lang hame,
Not here we'll meet again.
The kirk yard, the kirk yard,
Wi' flowr's o' every hue;
Shelter'd by the holly's shade,
And the dark sombre yew.

The settin' sun, the settin' sun,
How glorious it gaed doun;
The cloudy splendour raised our hearts
To cloudless skies aboon.
The auld dial, the auld dial,
It tauld how time did pass;
The wintry winds hae dang it doun,
Now hid 'mang weeds and grass.

Barbara Allan

It was in and ab - out the Mart' - mas time When the green leaves were a- fal - lin', That Sir John Graeme, in the west coun - try, Fell in love wi' Bar - b'ra Al - lan.

He sent his man down thro' the town To the place where she was dwal - lin'; 'O, haste and come to my mas - ter dear, Gin ye be Bar - b'ra Al - lan.'

O, hooly, hooly, rase she up,
To the place where he was lyin',
And when she drew the curtain by —
'Young man, I think ye're dyin'.'
'It's oh, I'm sick, I'm very sick,
And it's a' for Barbara Allan'
'O the better for me ye'se never be,
Though your heart's blude were a-spillin.'

O, dinna ye mind, young man,' she said
'When the red wine ye were fillin',
That ye made the healths gae round and round,
And slichtit Barb'ra Allan !'
He turn'd his face unto the wa',
And death was with him dealin';
'Adieu, adieu, my dear friends a',
And be kind to Barb'ra Allan.'

And slowly, slowly rase she up
And slowly, slowly left him
And sighin', said, she could not stay
Since death of life had reft him,
She hadna gane a mile but twa,
When she heard the deid-bell knellin'
And every jow the deid-bell gi'ed,
It cried, 'Wae to Barb'ra Allan.'

(as second part of the tune)
'Oh mother, mother, mak' my bed,
And mak' it saft and narrow;
Since my love died for me today,
I'll die for him tomorrow.'

47

To the Weavers Gin Ye Go

♩ = 100

My heart was ance as blythe and free As sim-mer days were lang; But a bon- nie, west- lin' wea- ver lad, Has gart me change my sang. To the wea- vers gin ye go, fair maid, To the wea- vers gin ye go, I rede ye right, gang ne'er at night, To the wea- vers gin ye go.

2 A bonnie, westlin weaver lad
Sat working at his loom;
He took my heart as wi' a net,
In every knot and thrum.

Chorus

3 I sat beside my warpin-wheel,
And aye I ca'd it roun';
But every shot and every knock,
My heart it gae a stoun.

Chorus

4 The moon was sinking in the west,
Wi' visage pale and wan,
And my bonnie, westlin weaver lad
Covoy'd me thro' the glen.

Chorus

5 But what was said, or what was done,
Shame fa' me gin I tell;
But Oh ! I fear the kintra soon
Will ken as weel's mysel !

Chorus

Rattlin' Roarin' Willie

♩. = 100

G

O rat- tlin', roar- in' Wil-lie, O he held to the fair, An'

G

for to sell his fid-dle and buy some i- ther ware; But

F

part- ing wi' his fid-dle the saut tear blin't his e'e; and

G   C   G   F   G

rat- tlin', roar- in' Wil-lie, ye're wel- come hame to me

'O Willie, come sell your fiddle,
O, sell your fiddle sae fine !
O Willie, come sell your fiddle,
And buy a pint o' wine !'
'If I should sell my fiddle,
The warld would think I was mad;
For monie a rantin day
My fiddle and I hae had.'

As I cam by Crochallan,
I cannilie keekit ben;
Rattlin', roarin' Willie
Was sittin' at your boord-en';
Sittin' at youn boord-en',
And amang gude company;
Rattlin', roarin' Willie,
Ye're welcome hame to me !

OMB 93

Maids When You're Young

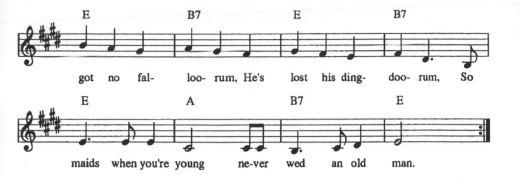

got   no   fal-   loo- rum, He's   lost   his ding-   doo- rum,   So

maids   when you're young   ne-ver   wed   an old   man.

Now, when we went to church, Hey ding a doorum down
Now, when we went to church, Hey doorum down
When we went to church, he left me in the lurch
Maids when you're young, never wed an auld man.

Chorus

Now, when we went to bed, Hey ding a doorum down
Now, when we went to bed, Hey doorum down
Now, when we went to bed, he lay like he was dead
Maids, when you're young, never wed an auld man.

Chorus

Now, when he went to sleep, Hey ding a doorum down
Now, when he went to sleep, Hey doorum down
Now, when he went to sleep, out of bed I did creep
Into the arms of a jolly young man.

Last Chorus:
And I found his fal-looral, fal-liddle, fal-looral,
I found his fal-looral, fal-diddle all day,
I found his fal loorum and he got my ding-doorum,
So maids, when you're young, never wed an auld man.

OMB 93

Jamie Foyers

♩ = 80

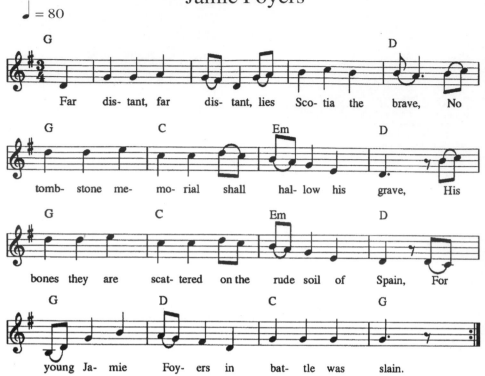

Far dis- tant, far dis- tant, lies Sco- tia the brave, No
tomb- stone me- mo- rial shall hal- low his grave, His
bones they are scat- tered on the rude soil of Spain, For
young Ja- mie Foy- ers in bat- tle was slain.

From the Perthshire Militia to serve in the line,
The brave Forty-second we sailed for to join.
To Wellington's army we did volunteer,
Along with young Foyers, that brave halberdier.

The night that we landed, the bugle did sound,
The general gave orders to form on the ground.
To storm Burgos Castle before break of day,
And young Jamie Foyers to lead on the way.

But mounting the ladder for scaling the wall,
By a shot from a French gun, young Foyers did fall,
He leaned his right arm upon his left breast,
And young Jamie Foyers his comrades addressed.

'For you Robert Percy, that stands a campaign,
If goodness should send you to Scotland again,
Please tell my old father if yet his heart warms,
That young Jamie Foyers expired in your arms.'

'But if a few moments in Campsie I were,
My mother and sisters my sorrow would share.
Now, alas, my old mother, long may she mourn,
But young Jamie Foyers will never return.'

'Oh ! if I could drink of Baker Brown's well,
My thirst it would quench and my fever would quell.'
But his very life-blood was ebbing so fast,
And young Jamie Foyers soon breathed his last.

They took for his winding sheet his ain tartan plaid,
And in the cold ground his body was laid.
With hearts full of sorrow they covered his clay,
And, saying 'Poor Foyers', marched slowly away.

His father and mother and sisters will mourn,
But Foyers, the brave hero, will never return.
His friends and his comrades lament for the brave,
Since young Jamie Foyers is laid in his grave.

The bugle may sound and war drum may rattle,
No more will they raise this young hero to battle.
He fell from the ladder a hero so brave,
And rare Jamie Foyers is lying in his grave.

OMB 93

Ae Fond Kiss

♩. = 54

Ae fond kiss and then we se-ver! Ae fare-well and then for-e-ver!

Deep in heart-wrung tears I'll pledge thee, war-ring sighs and grooms I'll wage thee.

I'll ne'er blame my partial fancy,
Naething could resist my Nancy:
But to see her was to love her;
Love but her and love for ever.
Had we never lov'd sae kindly,
Had we never lov'd sae blindly,
Never met–or never parted,
We had ne'er been broken-hearted.

Fare-thee-well, thou first and fairest !
Fare-thee-well, thou best and dearest !
Thine be ilka joy and treasure,
Peace, Enjoyment, Love and Pleasure !
Ae fond kiss, and then we sever !
Ae fareweel, alas, for ever !
Deep in heart-wrung tears I'll pledge thee,
Warring sighs and groans I'll wage thee.

Fareweel tae Tarwathie

♩ = 96

Fare - weel tae Tar - wa - thie, a - dieu, Mor - mond
Hill, And the dear land o' Crim - ond, I bid you fare
weel. I am bound now for Green - land and rea - dy to
sail, In hopes to find rich - es a- hunt ing the whale.

Our ship is weel-riggit and ready to sail
Our crew they are anxious to follow the whale
Where the icebergs do float and the stormy winds blaw
And the land and the ocean are covered wi' snaw.

The cold coast o' Greenland is barren and bare,
No seed-time nor harvest is ever known there,
And the birds here sing sweetly on mountain and dale,
But there isna a birdie tae sing tae the whale.

There is no habitation for a man to live there,
And the king of that country is the wild Greenland bear,
And there'll be no temptation to tarry long there,
With our ship bumper-fu' we will homeward repair.

Repeat first verse

OMB 93

Bonnie Dundee

 = 60

Dundee he is mounted, he rides up the street,
The bells they ring backward, the drums they are beat;
But the provost (douce man) said: 'Just e'en let it be,
For the toun is weel rid o' that deil o' Dundee'.

Chorus

'There are hills beyond Pentland, and lands beyond Forth,
Be there lords in the south, there are chiefs in the north;
There are brave Duinnewassals three thousand times three,
Will cry: 'Hey, for the bonnets o' Bonnie Dundee.'

Chorus

'Then awa' to the hills, to the lea, to the rocks,
Ere I own a usurper I'll crouch with the fox;
And tremble, false Whigs, in the midst o' your glee,
Ye hae no seen the last o' my bonnets and me.

Chorus

OMB 93

O Waly Waly

♩ = 100

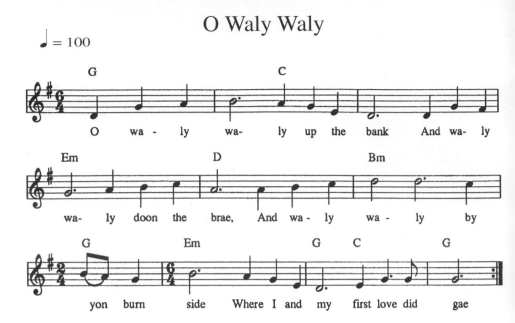

O wa - ly wa - ly up the bank And wa - ly
wa - ly doon the brae, And wa - ly wa - ly by
yon burn side Where I and my first love did gae

I leaned my back against an oak
Thinkin' it was a trusty tree,
But first it bent and then it broke,
And so did my first love tae me.

When we cam in frae Glasgow toun,
We were a comely sight tae see,
My love was clad in the velvet black,
And I mysel in cramasie.

Noo Arthur's Seat shall be my bed,
No sheets shall e'er be pressed by me,
Saint Anton's Well shall be my drink,
Since my fause love's forsaken me.

'Tis not the frost that freezes fell
Nor blawin' snaw's inclemency,
'Tis not sic cauld that makes me cry
But my love's heart's grown cauld tae me.

Oh Martinmas wind when wilt thou blaw
And shake the green leaves off the tree ?
Oh gentle death, when wilt thou come ?
For of my life I am weary.

Westering Home

♩ = 54

West - e- ring home, and a song in the air, Light in the eye, and it's

good - bye to care; Laugh- ter o' love, and a wel - com - ing there;

Isle of my heart, my own one! Tell me o' lands o' the

O- ri- ent gay! Speak o' the rich-es and joys o' Cath- ay! Eh, but it's grand to be

wa - kin' ilk day To find your - self near - er to Is - la. (And it's)

Chorus

Where are the folk like the folk o' the west ?
Canty and couthy and kindly, the best;
There I would hie me, and there I would rest
At hame wi' my ain folk in Isla. (And it's)

Chorus

OMB 93

There'll Never be Peace till Jamie Comes Hame

♩ = 104

By yon cast-le wa', at the close of the day, I heard a man sing, tho' his head it was grey; And as he was sing-ing, the tears doon came — There'll ne-ver be peace till Ja-mie comes hame.

The Church is in ruins, the State is in jars,
Delusions, oppresssions, and murderous wars,
We dare na weel say't, but we ken wha's to blame,–
There'll never be peace till Jamie comes hame.

My seven braw sons for Jamie drew sword,
But now I greet round their green beds in the yerd;
It brak the sweet heart o' my faithfu' auld dame,–
There'll never be peace till Jamie comes hame.

Now life is a burden that bows me down,
Sin' I tint my bairns, and he tint his crown;
But till my last moments my words are the same,–
There'll never be peace till Jamie comes hame.

A Brief Guide to the Songs

Although in no way meant to be comprehensive, the following notes will give as far as is relevant and traceable some idea of the background of each song in this volume. The brief glossaries with the notes contain some of the more obscure broad Scots expressions. In some cases, I have included explanations for words which will be obvious to any native Scot, but may need clarification for the sake of others.

5. CAM' YE O'ER FRAE FRANCE ?

The Hanoverian King George I brought with him a considerable entourage of courtiers, mistresses and aristocratic layabouts. 'Geordie Whelps' is the king himself. The 'goose' mentioned was his favourite mistress Madame Schulenberg. 'Bobbing John' refers to the Earl of Mar. This song as far as I could ascertain, does not appear in any old printed collection - possibly because of its embarrassing contents with regard to the origins of the British monarchy. It has appeared in a Manuscript dating back to the 18th century.

linkin — tripping along; claith — cloth; niffer — barter; wab — web; tint — lost; Ha's and mailins braid — houses and large estates; belyve — soon; hurdie — buttocks; skelp — slap

6. MAC PHERSON'S FAREWELL

Also known as MacPherson's rant. The story may be apocryphal, but there was apparently a notorious freebooter and fiddler by the name of James MacPherson, who was executed at the market cross of Banff in 1700. He is alleged to have composed this song and performed his final 'gig' standing under the noose and finishing with the ceremonial destruction of his instrument - so that 'nae ither hand shall play on thee, when I am dead and gone.' Robert Burns produced his own version of this song - as he did with hundreds of other Scottish songs and ballads. There is a version of this story in Katherine Briggs's Dictionary of British Folk Tales, called 'The Death of Singing Jamie.' I prefer to give you Ewan MacColl's version - which he in turn got from Jimmy McBeth of Elgin.

dee — die; sant — saint; afore — forwards; gie — give; brig — bridge; pit...afore — put the clock forward

8. LANG A-GROWING

Also known as 'The Bonny Boy' and 'My Bonnie Laddie's lang a-growin'. This song is known all over Britain and Ireland, and in Scotland first appeared in print as 'Lady Mary Ann' (Johnson 1792). The origin of the song lies in the marriage between a niece of the Bishop of Orkney and a much younger groom . This was more than likely an arranged marriage which served to unite land and properties of two families. The final verse seems abrasively casual about the ultimate fate of our lang growing teenager!

my lane — alone; lang — long; hae — have; muckle wrong — much wrong; ower — too; nae — no; fit — suit; abune my broo — above my brow; breeks — trousers; gang — go; sark — shirt; holland — linen; ain — own; aye — always/often; loot — lets; doon fa' — fall down

OMB 93

10. YE JACOBITES BY NAME
From Hogg's 'Jacobite Relics'. A slightly altered version appears in Johnson's (nr 371), this is from the pen of Robert Burns. According to Hogg the air is contemporaneous.

fautes — faults; mun — must

11. PLOOMAN LADDIES
Both the Gaberlunzie and Lucie Stewart have recorded this fine song. Sheila Douglas contributes: tp appreciate the way in which ploughmen, often called horsemen, were almost worshipped, you have to realise the status and pestige that was given to them by the Horseman's Word, a secret society into which they were all initiated. This was a mixtur e of practical horse management, magic and something bordering on trade unionism. A 'made horseman' was supposed to have special power over horses - and women!

doon — down; plooman — ploughman; sime — some; ain — own; verra — very; Cairt — cart; den — valley/ safe place; wisna — was not; widda...ill — would have made me sick; ilka — each/every; tae — to; stack — stack of peat/turf; hingin' — hanging; roon an' roon — round and round

12. ROTHESAY, O
This is a music hall parody written to an old song by William Watt, a weaver from Peebles (born 1792), who was also responsible for another well known ballad 'Kate Dalrymple'. It was published in the early 1900's and was originally called 'The Tinkler's Waddin'. Rothesay is where many Glaswegians went for their summer holidays long before the days of direct flights to Ibiza.

Hogmany — New Year's Eve; Glesca — Glasgow; sev'ral mair — several others; sodger — soldier; gaed — went; sic — such; cockit their lugs — cocked their ears; 'lope — dash

14. THE JOLLY BEGGAR
In some ways this song is similar to the 'Gaberlunzie Man' except that the tune is twice as lively. The beggar himself too seems more of a rascal and surely must have petrified the poor girl by blowing his horn and summoning his skippin', belted knights in the middle of the night. (I suspect other things may be meant by the second last verse.)

boun' — bound; wad — would; ahint — behind; e'en — evening; neuk — nook/corner; hooly — gently; loot a' his duddies fa' — let all his rags drop; brawest — most handsome

16. I'LL LAY YE DOON, LOVE
Also known as 'Inverey'. From the singing of Jeannie Robertson. Both words and music are of obscure origin, but certainly not older than the 19th century.
faur frae — far from

17. DUMBARTON'S DRUMS

The Earl of Dumbarton was commander of the Royal forces in Scotland during the reign of Charles II and James II. Hence the drums were those of a British regiment. The Earl distinguished himself by suppressing the rebellion of Argyle in 1685 and died in 1692. The song appeared in the 'Tea Table Miscellany' of 1724. The tune was originally known as 'I serve a Worthie Ladie.' (This information gleaned from G.F. Graham's 'Songs of Scotland Vol II, 1849). A song with the same title appears in 'Orpheus Caledonius' but words and tune are different.

caddie — messenger boy (perh. from cadet)

18. MAGGIE LAUDER

The tune of this lively song reminds one of the bagpipes, and it is indeed an air favoured by many players. The air was first recorded (as the vehicle for another song) in the 'Quakers Opera' performed in London in 1728. The words are by Francis Semple of Beltrees in Renfrewshire. Semple lived in the middle of the 17th century and wrote poetry, prose and songs such as 'She rose and let me in.' The Habbie Simpson mentioned was a famous piper from Killbarchan, Renfrewshire. Anster is short for Anstruther, a town in Fifeshire, where the famous 'Lint fair' was held annually.

wha wadna — who wouldn't; spier'd — asked/inquired; ca'd — called;
hallamshaker — worthless person/no-good; jog on your gate — be off with you;
bladderskate — silly, foolish person; fidgin' fain — very keen; winna steer — will not harm;
loup — jump/leap; brawly — well

19. HIELAND LADDIE

I drew a blank looking for other versions of this song. It may be an 18th or 19th century piece. What is known however, is that sailors sang another version of it - turned into a shanty. It is well-known in Canada under the name 'Donkey Riding,' and 'Hieland Laddie.' The words are quite different though:

> 'Were you ever in Quebec,
> Stowing timber on the deck,
> Where there's a king with a golden crown
> Riding on a donkey?'

Cargoes of timber were carried from Quebec in the 19th century into such ports as Glasgow where the sailors may have heard this song.

philabeg — kilt/plaid; trews — (tartan) trousers; a' — all; fa' — fall

20. LOCH TAY BOAT SONG

By Sir Harold Edwin Boulton (1859-1935), who edited many collections of Scottish, Irish and English folksongs such as the 'Skye Boat Song'. He generally borrowed from poetic and musical folklore and fashioned them into a new mould. Sometimes this worked well and has a charm of its own, at other times it might have been better to leave an old song as it was. The same

OMB 93

could be said of the many songs Burns collected and in some cases improved while on other occasions taking the heart out of the song.

nighean ruadh — (Gaelic for) red-haired darling; lint-white — flaxen fair

22. THE WEE, WEE GERMAN LAIRDIE
First printed in Cromek's 'Reliques of Nithsdale and Galloway Song' of 1810. The song reflects in a highly sarcastic manner the disdain with which the Scots regarded their new ruler, George I, the elector of Hanover.

wha the deil — who the devil; lairdie — a petty lord; gaed ower — went over; fouth — plenty; delvin in his kail yardie — digging in his cabbage garden; laying leeks — planting vegetables; breeks — trousers; beggar duds he cleeks — pulls up his beggar's rags; clappit doun — clapped down; brocht fouth — brought plenty; loons — knaves/no-goods; lang kail — tall cabbage; daur to pu' — dare to pull; haud — hold; mou — mouth; ower cauld a hole — too cold/inhospitable a place

24. THE BLUEBELLS OF SCOTLAND
According to Chappell (popular Music of the Olden Times), this song was composed (and sung) by a Mrs Jordan at the Theatre Royal, Drury Lane and was entered at Stationers' Hall on May 13, 1800. The air appears also in Thompson's collection of 1802. Nothing terribly Scots in its origins, but a popular song nonetheless.

25. THE REEL OF STUMPIE-O
From 'Songs of Scotland' by Allan Cunningham. As an actual reel it appears, with variations, in Niel Gow's Collection. The verses of this song are in Burns' 'Merry Muses', a collection of a generally frank nature.

hap and rowe — hop and roll/move and turn/ also : wrap (swaddling of a new born baby); feetie — little feet; greetie — a little cry; mankie — from calamanco - a kind of glossy woollen material; thumpin' quean — lively young woman; wi' dool an dumpie — with short but heavy steps; kimmer clash — chatting; caudle — cuddle; loon — rogue/ Aberdeenshire dialect for boy or young man; cutty stool — stool of repentance (in church, where those guilty of misconduct were obliged to sit); douce dames — kind ladies; sae dinna glower etc. — so don't you stare so glumly

26. THE GABERLUNZIE MAN
This song has been attributed to King James V, who apparently did have a penchant for dressing up (or down, rather) and mingling with the common folk to see what made them tick. Of course other monarchs too have been credited with the composition of many well known songs, notably 'Greensleeves' - supposedly penned by Henry VIII. The 'Gaberlunzie' or 'Beggarman' song first appears in Ramsays 'Tea Table Miscellany' of 1724. Gaberlunzies were licensed beggars who carried a leather pouch for collecting money or food.

tal' — told; wat — wet; cuist — cast/threw; mealpock — beggar's pack/bag; ayont — beyond; leal — faithful/honest (litt. loyal); claes — clothes; lain owre lang — overslept; rase — rose; gude gear gane — good things gone; kist — chest

28. CAULD KAIL IN ABERDEEN

The original of the song bears the date 1728 and refers to the Earl of Aberdeen, who died in 1720. A fair few subsequent adaptations followed, written by such luminaries as Alexander, fourth Duke of Gordon and Lady Nairne. Although our version is not the one which was highly rated in the last century I believe that the Duke of Gordon's (1743-1827) adaptation is very lively indeed. The Bogie is a river in Aberdeenshire.

castocks — cabbage stalks; cogie — wooden bowl; ding — push; wale — to choose;
rogie — dim. of rogue; vogie — cheerful; bang up the spring — start the reel;
pree their mou's — kiss; doited — silly; sae fain — so eager; hain — save;
maun hae their come — must have their turn; ilk ither — each other

29. THE PIPER O' DUNDEE

The tune of course is 'Aiken Drum'. The words are in Hogg's 'Jacobite Relics of Scotland'(1819-21). The references to the many Jacobite leaders mentioned suggests an 18th century origin. It has been put forward that the 'rogue' nature of the piper has a basis in history as there did exist a piper in Dundee by the name of Antonie Court who got himself into trouble by playing 'subversive' tunes. Amulrie is a village in Perthshire where the song indicates, a meeting was held to sort out the various allegiances. All the tunes mentioned are 18th century or earlier.

spring — reel; brent — brand; frac 'yont — from beyond; vow o' weir — declaration of war;
The Queer — the Choir

30. THE CALTON WEAVER

Ewan MacColl and other singers made this song very popular in the 60's. A longer version of it can be found in Ord's 'Bothy Ballads'. Ewan's condensed version came from the singing of Hughie Martin of Shettleston, Glasgow and was 'padded' with some of the verses from Ord. The 'whisky, whisky' bit seems a recent addition. Calton, a district of old Glasgow, used to be famous for its weavers' workshops.

siller — silver; heid — head (pron. heed); whit's the lawin — what's the expense;
scale — sixpence

32. O CAN YE SEW CUSHIONS ?

A gentle old lullabye. It appears in Johnson's 'Scots Musical Museum', where it was contributed by Robert Burns. This was one of the many songs that Burns collected and in some cases completed or adapted.

greets — cries; mony o' ye — (so) many of you; biggit — built; sair — mournful (litt. sore);
saut — salt

OMB 93

34. ANNIE LAURIE

The original words were written as a poem by a Douglas of Fingland, who indeed was smitten by Annie Laurie, a daughter of Sir Robert Laurie, first baronet of Maxwellton. It is likely that these verses were written around the close of the 17th century. The unfortunate poetic wooer never gained his prize as she married a Mr. Ferguson of Craigdarroch. The air of the song is much more recent and was adapted by Lady Scott in the early 19th century.

fa's — falls; doon/doun — down; dee — die; gowan — the wild daisy; fa' o' her etc. — tread of her

35. A MAN'S A MAN FOR A' THAT

It is known that Burns harboured republican feelings and frequently spoke in favour of the French and American Revolutions. Society and the class-system in particular was for the first time ever perceived as something unfair and to be improved upon. The great classic essay on democracy, 'The Rights of Man' by Tom Paine, was published in England in 1791. Burns own opinion of this song (written in 1794) was rather subdued: 'I fear for my songs, however, a few may please, yet originality is a coy feature in composition, and in multiplicity of efforts in the same style, disappears altogether. A great critic (Aikin) on song says, that love and wine are the exclusive themes for song-writing. The following is on neither subject, and consequently is no song, but will be allowed, I think, to be two or three pretty good prose thoughts inverted into rhyme.' The tune appears in 1759 in Bremner's 'Scots Reels' as 'Lady McIntosh's Reel'.

a' — all; gowd — gold; hoddin grey — coarse homespun cloth; birkie — a conceited fellow; coof — fool/twit; aboon — above; maunna fa' that — must/may not do that (it is beyond his power) ; pith — force/strength; bear the gree — be victorious

36. THE BONNIE LASS O' FYVIE O

Greig's Collection features a great many variants of this well-known song from different contributors throughout Scotland. Our version here was taken from a variety of sources. Greig's fine collection has no less than 26 variants in music and lyrics and apart from that there are numerous recordings with other versions - many of these condensed ones, to make them suitable for today's impatient audiences. What I've given here is what seems to me a version that may come close to the original. Oral tradition is wonderful thing which will often improve a song or story, at other times however the sense of certain phrases and a sequence of events may get muddled up and get carried on forever. I've tried my utmost to combine verses as sung by different singers into an integrated singable song. 'Bonnie Barbara O' is an English version of this song, and I recall a recording by Bob Dylan with the Appalachian equivalent - 'Pretty Peggy.'

yellow hair — blonde hair; flounces — frills; minnie — mother; sodger — soldier; birks — birch trees

38. JOCKEY'S TA'EN THE PARTING KISS
Written to the air 'Bonie lass tak a man'. Although intended for Johnson's 'Museum' this work was actually published in Dr. Currie's editions of Burns. The word jockey here has little to do with horse-racing, it is simply the old generic term for a man/chap/fellow.

39. CHARLIE IS MY DARLING
Burns sent an early version of this song to Johnson for inclusion in 'The Museum'. A second version was written by Hogg, for his 'Jacobite Reliques'. A third and fourth adaptation were effected by Captain Charles Gray and Stephen Clarke. The latter was the Edinburgh organist and friend of Robert Burns. Our version though features the words of Lady Nairne.

claymores — highlanders' large two-edged sword

40. TAE THE BEGGIN' I WILL GO
Fitted with a variety of tunes this lively song has been around for a while and represents with 'The Gaberlunzie Man' a type of song, illustrating the popular image of the mendicant of old. The words given here are 'version O' as recorded by Gavin Greig around the turn of the century. A song, dating back to the 18th century is 'There was a Jovial Beggar', which shares the chorus and some of the verses of 'Tae the Beggin' and may have been its predecessor.

aye   always; inhy — inside; gin ye gie — if you give; bree   barley brew/whiskey; kale — cabbage; picklemeal — a bit of meal (corn); brose and kail — oatmeal and cabbage; bawbees — small coins; dae — do

42. THE BONNIE EARL O' MORAY
(Child 181) This song only appears in a few printed sources. When it does, it yields no more information than 'old Scottish Song' or 'Traditional Melody,' and it's impossible to even guess a date. The events described in the narrative are clear enough: towards the end of the sixteenth century a great power struggle was taking place around the court of James VI (1566-1625). Royal authority was under threat from various quarters, but the so-called 'Northern Earls' were the most obvious protagonists who had managed to stay clear of subjugation to any extent. Court intrigues and difficulties in containing the headstrong Gaelic earls may have led to the assassination of James Stewart, the Earl of Moray at the hand of the Earl of Huntly on Feb 7th 1592. The song implies an amorous connection between the Queen (Anne of Denmark) and Moray, which may well be fictitious.

calland — youth

OMB 93

43. THE BAND O' SHEARERS
The tune is the very same as is used in the Ulster song 'The Rollicking Boys Around Tandaragee'. Paddy Tunney (on Ossian OSS 74) sings a wonderful version of this song. As to the origins of this Scottish (possibly bothy) ballad, I am very much in the dark.

owre — too

44. THE AULD HOOSE
Written by Lady Nairne (1766-1845). The tune may be either her own, or possibly Nathaniel Gow's. The lyrics are in the form of a private reminiscing of Lady Nairne's own birthplace, the old house of Gask in Perthshire. The 'Bonnie Earn' refers to the river nearby. The Irish author and playwright Sean O'Casey produced a song for one of his plays called 'Since Maggie went away', which is set to the music of this song.

bairnies — babes/children; reca' — recall; canty — cheerful; crouse — confident; leddy — lady; tauld — told; dang it doun — knocked it down

46. BARBARA ALLAN
A song of venerable antiquity: Pepys, in his diary mentions that on January 2, 1666 he heard his 'Dear Mrs. Knipp sing her little Scotsh song of Barbary Allan'. The song is also well known in its American adaptation: 'In Scarlet town, where I was born' etc. - although this is practically another song, the words and music being radically different. Printed versions occur in Child (84), Ramsay's 'Miscellany' of 1724, and others.

Mart'mas — Martinmas - the 11th of November; hooly — slowly; rase — rose; ye'se — you will; slichtit — slighted; reft — bereft; deid-bell — bell tolling for the dead; jow — toll/swing of bell; wae — woe

48. TO THE WEAVERS GIN YE GO
From the quill of Robert Burns. Possibly an adaptation of an already existing song. One of the liveliest and sprightliest songs in this collection. Very few of Burns' sources mention this fine song and its history is quite obscure when compared against the certified masses of information relating to most of his songs and poems.

ance — once; simmer — summer; westlin' — from the West; gart — made; sang —song; gin — if/should; rede — advise; gang — go; warp — weave; wab — weft/cloth; sab — sob; thrum — end of a warp thread (waste) ; aye — always; ca'd it roun — turned it around; gae a stoun — (lit.) gave a (severe) ache; fa' me — befall me; kintra — country

49. RATTLIN' ROARIN' WILLIE
William Dunbar was esteemed to be 'one of the worthiest fellows in the world' by Burns when he adapted and lengthened this old song with its final stanza. Burns was a leading member of a convivial bachelors club in

Edinburgh, the Crochallan Fencibles, which was presided over by Mr. Dunbar.

ither ware — other things; saut — salt; blin't his e'e — blinded his eye; rantin — lively/noisy; cannilie keekit ben — cautiously looked (peeked) inside; boord-en — table (board)-end

50. MAIDS WHEN YOU'RE YOUNG
Versions of this saucy song abound all over Britain and Ireland. Recordings of it were made by, amongst others, Jeannie Robertson in Aberdeen and Sam Larner in Norfolk. Printed versions occur in Herd's of 1870, Kidson's of 1891 and Petrie of 1902.

52. JAMIE FOYERS
From Ford's 'Vagabond Songs and Ballads'. Ford states that this song was very popular in rural Perthshire before and about the middle of the 1900's. There really was a Sergeant James Foyer, who was born in Campsie, Stirlingshire and was killed at the siege of Burgos in 1812. Ewan MacColl produced a re-written version of this song to commemorate the Spanish Civil War.

54. AE FOND KISS
Written by Robert Burns. Walter Scott felt that: 'these exquisitely affecting stanzas contain the essence of a thousand love tales.' It is believed that this song relates to the poet's parting with his 'Clarinda' whose real name was Mrs. Agnes McLehose and whose relationship with Burns appeared to be the only one he managed to keep platonic. The air 'Rory Dall's Port' is an ancient harp tune attributed to the blind harper Dall, who was born on the Isle of Lewis around 1600. A great deal of variants exist of this air and over the years 'Ae Fond Kiss' was - apparently by popular choice - slightly changed away from the air to which the words were set originally. One version appears in Captain Fraser's 'Collection of Airs and Melodies Peculiar to the Highlands' (1816), where it is printed as 'The Cow-Boy'.

ae — a; nae — no; ilka — every

55. FAREWEEL TAE TARWATHIE
Words by George Scroggie, a miller by trade who lived at Federate in New Deer Parish in the 19th century. The song was collected by A.L. Lloyd from the singing of John Sinclair of Ballater. Many men went to sea to hunt the sperm whale in vast operations that have (mercifully) slowly ground to a virtual halt over the last 25 years or so. The lyrics and general contents of this song are quite similar in style to those of the Irish/Scottish song 'The Greenland Whale Fisheries'.

blaw — blow; snaw — snow

OMB 93

56. BONNIE DUNDEE

The Dundee of this song is not the town of that name, but the rebel Viscount of Dundee, Graham Claverhouse. (see 'Killiecrankie'). Although the modern words are by Sir Walter Scott - from 'The doom of Dervogoil' - there did exist an old version of this song, which was first published in D'Urfey's 'Pills to Purge Melancholy' of 1719. That song was called 'Jockey's Escape from Dundee' and was set to the air 'Adew Dundee.' The present air, according to Moffat, may have been composed by Charlotte Sainton-Dolby in the 19th century. It is a fine strong air, with a marching feel about it making it a favourite with military bands.

douce — kind/dear; e'en — here: might as well; Duinnewassals — (anglicised Gaelic for) gentlemen

58. O WALY WALY

First printed in 'The Orpheus Caledonius' (1725), this song relates the story of Lady Barbara Erskine, daughter of the ninth Earl of Mar, who married James, second marquis of Douglas in 1670. She was falsely accused of adultery by an ex-lover. The ballad takes the form of a lament of the poor lady and it must have been a very popular item at the time - songs and ballads relating such stories of scandal and betrayal really are the very ancestors of today's tabloids. An American version of this song, but with a different tune exists in 'The Water is Wide'.

waly — (here) expression of grief (poss. woe); cramasie — crimson cloth (perh. satin); fause — false

59. WESTERING HOME

Words by Hugh S. Roberton (1874-1952), who together with Marjory Kennedy-Fraser and Granville Bantock collected and arranged many Hebridean tunes and songs. Roberton himself led a musically involved lifestyle, ranging from organising a choir made up out of Glasgow street urchins to his wonderful arrangements of songs such as 'Lewis Bridal Song', 'Mingulay Boat Song' and others. He also produced the well-known 'All in the April Evening' and many other original compositions and arrangements. His involvement in the Gaelic movement in Scotland brought about his friendship with Kenneth McLeod, Kennedy-Fraser's literary collaborator, as well as with political figures such as DeValera. He was one of the founder governors of the Scottish Royal Academy of Music and Drama. The first half of the song resembles 'Bonny Strathyre,' but actually derives from the Gaelic song 'Eilean Mo Chridh', while the second half was composed by Roberton himself . Roberton was knighted for his services to music in 1931.

canty — neat; couthy — homely

60. THERE'LL NEVER BE PEACE TILL JAMIE COMES HAME

The tune is: 'There are few good fellows when Jamie's awa' as published in Oswalds 'Collection of Curious Scots Tunes' (1742). Also known as ' By Yon Castle Wa'. Robert Burns had come across only the title of this song and he seized the opportunity to craft it into a stirring, patriotic song in the Jacobite tradition. All the memories of mishaps and wrongdoings of the political and military events scarcely two generations earlier were still very much alive around the time when Burns wrote these verses.

wa' — wall; greet — weep; Sin' I tint — As I lost

OMB 93

Published by
OSSIAN PUBLICATIONS
14-15 Berners Street, London W1T 3LJ, UK.

Exclusive distributors:
MUSIC SALES LIMITED
Distribution Centre, Newmarket Road,
Bury St Edmunds, Suffolk, IP33 3YB, UK.

MUSIC SALES CORPORATION
257 Park Avenue South, New York, NY 10010
United States Of America.

MUSIC SALES PTY LIMITED
20 Resolution Drive, Caringbah,
NSW 2229, Australia.

OMB 93
ISBN 978-0-946005-78-8
This book © Copyright 1994, 2002, 2008 by
Novello & Company Limited,
part of The Music Sales Group.

Design and Lay-out by John Loesberg
Production Assistant and Typesetting by Grace O'Halloran
Painting on cover reproduced by permission of the National Galleries
of Scotland: (Detail from) The Porteous Mob by James Drummond.
Special thanks to the staff of the National Library of Scotland, Edinburgh.
Westering Home © Roberton Publications
Specal thanks to Kenneth Roberton

Special thanks to Sheila Douglas

Printed in the EU.

www.musicsales.com

Other titles in this series:
Traditional Folksongs & Ballads of Scotland Vol 2
OMB 94   ISBN 0 946005 79 6
Traditional Folksongs & Ballads of Scotland Vol 3
OMB 95   ISBN 0 946005 80 X
The Scottish Songs of Robert Burns
OMB 96   ISBN 0 946005 81 8